CHI

Reading
BOROUGH COUNCIL

Reading Borough Libraries

Email: info@readinglibraries.org.uk
Website: www.readinglibraries.org.uk

Reading 0118 9015950
Battle 0118 9015100
Caversham 0118 9015103
Palmer Park 0118 9015106
Southcote 0118 9015109
Tilehurst 0118 9015112
Whitley 0118 9015115

Author: MORPURGO, Michael
Title: Little Foxes

Class no.

To avoid overdue charges please return this book to a
Reading library ~~c~~ ove.
If not required b by
personal visit, tel site.

D1421905

LITTLE FOXES

Michael Morpurgo

First published in Great Britain in 1984
by Kaye & Ward Ltd
This Large Print edition published by
BBC Audiobooks Ltd 2008
by arrangement with
Egmont Books Ltd

ISBN: 978 1405 662727

British Library Cataloguing in Publication Data available

Printed and bound in Great Britain by
CPI Antony Rowe, Chippenham, Wiltshire

For Basty, Ration and Ross.

CHAPTER ONE

Billy Bunch came in a box one wintry night ten years ago. It was a large box with these words stencilled across it: 'Handle with care. This side up. Perishable.'

For Police Constable William Fazackerly this was a night never to be forgotten. He had pounded the streets all night checking shop doors and windows, but it was too cold a night even for burglars. As he came round the corner and saw the welcome blue light above the door of the Police Station, he was thinking only of the mug of sweet hot tea waiting for him in the canteen. He bounded up the steps two at a time and nearly tripped over the box at the top.

At first it looked like a box of flowers, for a great bunch of carnations—blue from the light above—filled it from end to end. He crouched down and parted the flowers. Billy lay there swathed in blankets up

1

to his chin. A fluffy woollen bonnet covered his head and ears so that all Police Constable Fazackerly could see of him were two wide open eyes and a toothless mouth that smiled cherubically up at him. There was a note attached to the flowers: 'Please look after him', it read.

Police Constable Fazackerly sat down beside the box and tickled the child's voluminous cheeks and the smile broke at once into a giggle so infectious that the young policeman dissolved into a high-pitched chuckle that soon brought the Desk Sergeant and half the night shift out to investigate. The flowers—and they turned white once they were inside—were dropped unceremoniously into Police Constable Fazackerly's helmet, and the child was borne into the Station by the Desk Sergeant, a most proprietary grin creasing his face. 'Don't stand there gawping,' he said. 'I want hot water bottles, lots of 'em and quickly. Got to get him warm; and Fazackerly, you phone for the doctor and tell him it's urgent. Go on, lad, go

on.' And it was the same Desk
Sergeant who to his eternal credit
named the child, not after himself, but
after the young Police Constable who
had found him. 'I've named a few waifs
and strays in my time,' he said, 'and I'll
not condemn any child to carry a name
like Fazackerly all his life. But Billy

3

he'll be—not Billy Carnation, he'd never forgive us—no. Now let me see, how about Billy Bunch for short? How's that for a name, young feller-me-lad?' And Billy giggled his approval.

Billy did not know it, but that moment in his box on the table in the Interrogation Room with half a dozen adoring policemen bending over him was to be his last taste of true contentment for a long time. He was not to know it either, but he sent a young policeman home that night to his bed with his heart singing inside him. Billy Bunch was a name he was never to forget.

Billy Bunch was taken away to hospital and processed from there on. First there was the children's home where he stayed for some months whilst appeals and searches were carried out to see if anyone would claim him. No one did. In all that time he had only one visitor. Once a week on his afternoon off Police Constable William Fazackerly would come and sit by his cradle, but as the months passed the child seemed to recognise him less and less, and would cry now when he reached out to touch him. So, because he felt he was making the child unhappy, he stopped coming.

By his first birthday Billy Bunch had entirely lost the smile he had come with. A grim seriousness overshadowed him and he became pensive and silent, and this did nothing to endear him to the nurses who, try as they did, could find little to love in the child. Neither was he an attractive boy. Once he had lost the chubby charm of his infancy, his ears were seen to stick out more than they should and they could find no parting for his hair which would never lie down.

He did not walk when it was expected of him, for he saw no need to. He remained obstinately impervious to either bribes or threats and was quite content to shuffle around on his bottom for the first two and a half years of his life, one leg curled underneath him acting as his rudder, thumb deep in his mouth and forefinger planted resolutely up his left nostril.

And speech did not come easily to him as it did with other children in the home. Even the few words he spoke refused to leave his mouth without his having to contort his lips and spit them out. This stutter made him all the more reluctant to communicate and he turned to pictures and eventually, when he could read, to books for comfort.

No foster family, it seemed, wanted to keep him for long; and each time his case was packed again to return to the children's home, it simply confirmed that he was indeed alone and unwanted in this world.

School made it worse if anything. The frequent changes from one foster home to another spoiled any chances he might have had of making firm friends in those early years. And certainly he was not proving to be a favourite with the teachers. He was not bright in the classroom, but most of the teachers could forgive him that. The trouble was that he seemed completely uninterested and made little attempt to disguise it. All he wanted to do was to read, but he would never read what they wanted him to read.

And with his fellows he was no more popular, for he was neither strong nor agile and had little stomach for competitive games of any kind. At play time he would wander alone, hands deep in his pockets, his brows furrowed. The other children were no more beastly to him than they were to each other, in fact they paid him scant attention. Were it not for his stutter he would have gone through each day at school almost unnoticed.

Mrs Simpson, or Aunty May as she liked to be called, was the latest in the long line of foster mothers. She had thin lips, Billy noticed, that she made up bright scarlet to look like a kiss, and she wore curlers every Sunday night in her fuzzy purple hair. She was a widow with grown-up children who lived away. She kept a clean enough house on the tenth floor of a block of flats that dominated that wind-swept estate on the outskirts of the city. The estate had been built after the War to accommodate the workers needed for

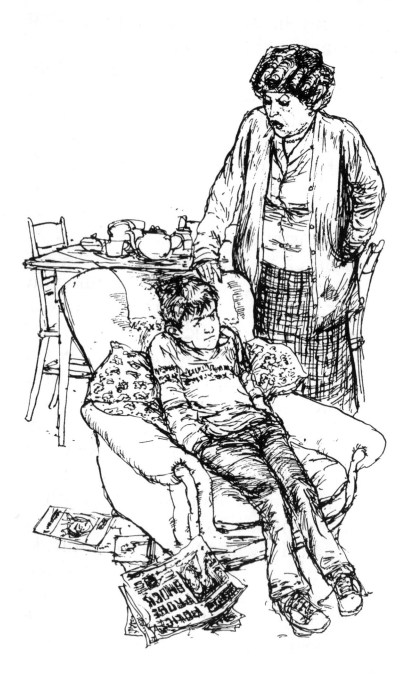

the nearby motor factory, and accommodate was all it did. It was tidily organised with rank upon rank of identical box houses, detached and semi-detached, spread out like a giant spider's web around the central block of flats where Billy now lived. There was little grass to play on and what there was was forbidden to him because he might get muddy, and Aunty May did not like that. 'After all, you know,' she was continually reminding him, 'they only give me so much to keep you each week, Billy, and I can't be for ever spending on extra washing just because you go out and get yourself in a state. I can't think why you don't go and play in the adventure playground with the other children. It's all concrete there, and much better for you. It's not fair on me, Billy, not fair at all. I've told you before, Billy, if you can't do as you're told, you'll have to go.'

That was always the final threat, and not one to which Billy was usually susceptible, for most of his foster homes had meant little more to him than a roof over his head and three meals a day. Seen like that, one such home was much like any other. But this home was the only one that had ever been special to him. This one he wanted very much to stay in, not on account of Aunty May who nagged him incessantly, and certainly not on account of the school where he lived in dread of the daily torture Mr Brownlow, his frog-eyed teacher, inflicted upon him. 'Stand up, Billy,' he would say. 'Your turn now. Stand up and read out the next page, aloud. And don't take five minutes about it, lad. Just do it.' And so he did it, but the inevitable sniggers as he stuttered his way through added yet more tissue to the scar of hurt and humiliation he tried so hard to disguise. No, he endured all that and Aunty May only because he had his Wilderness down by the canal to which he could escape and be at last amongst friends.

CHAPTER TWO

The chapel of St Cuthbert, or what was left of it, lay in the remotest corner of the estate, a gaunt ancient ruin that was crumbling slowly into oblivion. Like everything else standing on the site it would have been bulldozed when the estate was built, but a preservation order had ensured its survival—no one was quite sure why. So they erected a chain-link fence around the graveyard that surrounded the ruins and put up a warning sign: 'Keep out. Danger of falling masonry.' And, for the most part, the children on the estate did keep out, not because of the sign—few of them knew what masonry was anyway—but rather because it was common knowledge that there were ghosts roaming around the graveyard. And the few who had ventured through the wire and into the Wilderness beyond returned with stories of strange rustlings in the undergrowth, footsteps that followed them relentlessly, and head-high whispering nettles that lashed at intruders as they tried to escape. This was enough to discourage all but the most adventurous children.

Billy was by no means adventurous, but he no longer believed in ghosts and

like most children he had always been intrigued by anything that was forbidden. He was on one of his solitary evening wanderings shortly after he came to live with Aunty May when he saw a great white owl fly over his head and into the vaulted ruins. It passed so close to him that he could feel the wind of its wings in his hair. He saw it settle on one of the arched windows high up in the ruins. It was because he wanted a closer look that he pulled up the rusty wire and clambered into the Wilderness.

Since that first evening Billy had returned every day to his Wilderness; skulking along the wire until he was sure no one would see him go in, for the magic of this place would be instantly shattered by any intrusion on his privacy. He would dive under the wire, never forgetting to straighten it up behind him so that no one would ever discover his way in, and would fight his way through the undergrowth of laurels and yew out into the open graveyard. Hidden now from the estate, and with the world wild about him, Billy at last found peace. Here he could lie back on the springy grass the rabbits had cropped short and soft, and watch the larks rising into the sky until they vanished into the sun. Here he could keep a lookout for his owls high in the stone wall of the chapel itself, he could laugh out loud at the sparrows' noisy warfare, call back at the insistent call of the greenfinch and applaud silently the delicate dance of the wagtails on the gravestones.

In the evenings, if he lay quite still for long enough, the rabbits would emerge tentative from their burrows and sniff for danger, and how his heart leapt with the compliment they paid him by ignoring him. No need ever to bring his books here. It was enough for him to be a part of this paradise. He did not need to know the name of a red admiral butterfly or a green woodpecker in order to enjoy their beauty. He came to know every bird, every creature, that frequented his Wilderness and looked upon them as his own. In spring he took it upon himself to guard the fledglings against the invasion of predatory cats from the estate. A stinging shot from his catapult was usually sufficient to deter them from a return visit. He was lord of his Wilderness, its guardian and its keeper.

Beyond the chapel was the canal. The ruin itself and the graveyard were screened on that side by a jungle of willows and alder trees, and nearer the canal by a bank of hogweed and foxgloves. Hidden here, Billy could watch unobserved as the moorhens and coots jerked their way through the still water, their young scooting after them.

But his greatest joy was the pair of brilliant kingfishers that flashed by so fast and so straight that at first Billy thought he had imagined them. All that summer he watched them come and go. He was there when the two young were learning to fish. He was there when the four of them sat side by side no more than a few feet from him, their blazing orange and blue unreal against the greens and browns of the canal banks. Only the dragonflies and damselflies gave them any competition; but for Billy the kingfishers would always be the jewels of his Wilderness.

One summer's evening he was kingfisher-watching by the canal when he heard the sound of approaching voices and the bark of a dog on the far side of the canal, and this was why he was lying hidden, face down in the long grass when the cygnet emerged from the bulrushes. She cruised towards him, surveying the world about her with a look of mild interest and some disdain. Every now and then she would browse through the water, lowering her bill so that the water lapped gently over it, then her head would disappear completely until it re-emerged, dripping. Although a dark blue-grey,

16

the bill tinged with green, she looked already a swan in the making. No other bird Billy knew of swam with such easy power. No other bird could curve its neck with such supreme elegance. Billy hardly dared to breathe as the cygnet moved effortlessly towards him. She was only a few feet away now and he could see the black glint of her eye. He was wondering why such a young bird would be on its own and was waiting for the rest of the family to appear when the question was unequivocally answered.

'That's one of 'em,' came a voice from the opposite bank of the canal. 'You remember? We shelled them four swans, made 'em fly, didn't we? 'S got to be one of 'em. Let's see if we can sink him this time. Let's get him.' In the bombardment of stones that followed Billy put his hands over his head to protect himself. He heard most of the stones falling in the water but one hit him on the arm and another landed limply on his back. Outrage drove away his fear and he looked up to see five youths hurling a continuous barrage of stones at the cygnet who beat her wings in a frantic effort to take off, but the bombardment was on the mark and she was struck several times leaving her stunned, bobbing up and down helpless in the turbulent water. The dog they launched into the river was fast approaching, its black nose ploughing through the water towards the cygnet, and Billy knew at once what had to be done. He picked up a dead branch and leapt out into the water between the dog and cygnet. Crying with fury he lashed out at the dog's head and drove it back until it clambered whimpering up the bank to join its masters. With abuse ringing in his ears and the stones falling all around him Billy gathered up the battered cygnet in his arms and made for the safety of the Wilderness. The bird struggled against him but Billy had his arms firmly around the wings and hung on tight.

Once inside the ruins Billy sank to his knees and set the cygnet down beside him. One of her wings trailed on the ground as she staggered away and

it appeared she could only gather it up with some difficulty. For a moment she stood looking around her, wondering. Then she stepped out high and pigeon-toed on her wide webbed feet and marched deliberately around the chapel. She shook herself vigorously, opened out and beat both her wings, and then settled down at some distance from Billy to preen herself. Shivering, Billy hugged himself and drew his knees up to keep out the cold of the evening. He was not going to leave until he was sure the cygnet was strong enough to go back in the canal. He sat in silence for some minutes, still simmering with anger, but his anger vanished as he considered the young swan in front of him. He started speaking without thinking about it.

'Must be funny to be born grey and turn white after,' he said. 'Not a bit like an ugly duckling, you aren't. Most beautiful thing I've ever seen—so you can't hardly be ugly, can you? Course you're not as beautiful now as you're going to be, but I 'spect you know that. You'll grow up just like your mother, all white and queenly.' And the cygnet stopped preening herself for a moment and looked sideways at him. 'Did they kill your mother too, then?' Billy asked. 'They did, didn't they? What did they do it for? I hate them. I hate them. Well I'll look after you now. You got to keep close in to the bank whenever you see anyone—don't trust anyone, I never do—and I'll come by each day and bring some bread with me. I'm called Billy, by the way, Billy Bunch, and I'm your friend. Wish you could speak to me, then I'd know you can understand what I'm telling you. And you could tell me a few things yourself, couldn't you? I mean, you could tell me how to fly for a start. You could teach me, couldn't you?' And suddenly Billy was aware that his words were flowing easily with not so much as a trace of a stutter. 'Teach, teach, teach, teach . . .' Billy repeated the word each time, spitting out the T. 'But I stutter on my T's, always have done. T's and P's and C's—can't never get them out. But I can now, I can now. Never mind the flying, you've taught me to speak. I can

21

speak, I can talk. Billy Bunch can talk. He can talk the hind leg off a horse.' And Billy was on his feet and cavorting around the chapel in a jubilant dance of celebration, laughing till the tears ran down his cheeks. He shouted out every word he could remember that had ever troubled him and every word he shouted buried more deeply the stutter he had lived with all his life. By the time he had finished he was breathless and hoarse. He turned at last to where the cygnet had been standing but she had vanished.

Billy searched the Wilderness from end to end. He retraced the path to the canal but there was no sign of her. He found only one small grey feather left behind on the grassy floor of the chapel where the cygnet had been preening herself. This and the fact that he was still soaked to the skin from the canal was enough to convince Billy he had not been dreaming it all. As he made his way home across the darkening estate, the blue-white lights of the television sets flickering through the curtains, he practised the words and they still flowed.

He expected and received dire admonitions and warnings from Aunty May who railed against little boys in general and the price of washing powder in particular before sending him to bed early. Billy smiled to himself in his bed, hid his grey feather under the pillow and when he slept he dreamed dreams of swans or angels—he was not sure which.

When Billy's turn came the next morning to read his page out aloud in class, he stood up and looked about him deliberately at the already sniggering children before he began. Then, using his grey feather to underline the words, he began in a clear lucid voice to read. Mr Brownlow took the glasses from his frog-eyes in disbelief, and every smirk in the classroom was wiped away as Billy read on faultlessly to the end of the page. 'You may sit down now, Billy' was all Mr Brownlow could say when he had finished. 'Yes, that was very good, Billy, very good indeed. You may sit down.' And the silence around him, born of

23

astonishment and grudging respect, soaked in through Billy's skin and warmed him to the bone.

CHAPTER THREE

Aunty May was ecstatic about Billy's miraculous cure from his stutter. Of course she had her own theory about the cause of this, and was not slow to voice it to anyone who would listen. 'I've always said that a happy home is the best cure for all evils. That's all Billy needed, a happy, loving home; and he's not the first, you know. Oh no, Billy will be the fifth foster child I've looked after since my own boys grew up and went away. And he's a lovely boy, one of the best I've had. You know, no one else would take him. Well, poor little mite, I suppose he's not much to look at, is he? But I don't mind that. Eats me out of house and home but we mustn't think of that, must we? And dirty? Is he dirty? You should see the state he gets in. But there we are. Boys will be boys. After all we don't do it for the money, do we?'

And the school too claimed

responsibility for Billy's new-found voice. Mr Brownlow was congratulated by the Head Teacher at the end-of-term Staff Meeting. 'Quite a job you've done there, Mr Brownlow,' she said. 'Should give Billy new confidence— and the Speech Therapist had quite given up on him you know. Any idea how you managed the impossible, Mr Brownlow?'

'It's a slow process of course,' said Mr Brownlow, nodding knowingly. 'All education is you know. But I'd say patience had something to do with it. Yes, patience and faith in one's own tried and proved methods. They love to get up and read you know. All the others were reading well, and I suppose he didn't want to be different. I mean, who does? That's what did it I expect. Yes, I do believe he was shamed into it.'

But the self-righteous glow at home and school soon faded as it was realised that Billy did not wish to use his new voice. He remained as silent and withdrawn as ever, speaking only when he had to and then briefly. At school he would spend hours staring at the distant trees of his Wilderness through the classroom window, chewing the end of his pencil. His confidential report read: 'Very much below average intelligence. He always seems to want to be somewhere else. Not a good prospect.'

At home Aunty May had discovered that to threaten to send him away did indeed bring Billy back home before dark, did bring him in on time for meals. And she was not too bothered what he got up to in between times just so long as he did not get into any trouble or get his clothes dirty. 'I'll keep him on for a while, but I don't like the child,' she told the Social Worker on one of his rare visits.

'Who does?' came the reply.

During that winter, whenever he was not in school, Billy spent every hour of daylight in his Wilderness. He often thought of playing truant and would have done so but he knew Aunty May would have him back inside the children's home the next day if he started that. So immediately school was

over every afternoon he would make
for the Wilderness, his duffle bag full
of the scraps he had secreted in his
pockets during school dinner. It was a
hard winter that year. The ground
froze in late November and the first
snow came early in December. Billy
saw himself as the protector of all the
wild things in his Wilderness. He would
spread his scraps evenly throughout the
Wilderness and then watch them feed.
Rampaging rooks and slow crows came
wheeling in first and he would drive

them away with his catapult so as to allow the smaller birds first pickings— the robins and the hedge-sparrows and

the blackbirds. But he could do nothing for the barn owls, nor for the family of kingfishers. He tried. He purloined sardines from Aunty May's larder but the kingfishers ignored them. He took some of Aunty May's stew and put it out on a gravestone for the owls but they never came for it. He broke the ice on the canal each day so that the kingfishers could fish, but it froze over almost as he watched. He had to stand by and see them weaken as the winter wore on.

And he had not forgotten his swan; he looked for her every day and searched the canal bank for her feathers. He threw bread out onto the canal to attract her back, but there was never any sign of her.

Then one day—it was just after Christmas—the owls were no longer in their arched window in the high stone wall of the ruin and that same day he found a kingfisher lying stiff and dead by the canal. He could see it was one of the young ones for it still had a white tip to its beak and a mottled breast. The ground was too hard to bury it so he carried it reverently in his hands down to the canal, hammered a hole in the ice and slipped it into the water. He could not cry—he was too angry for that. As he watched it disappear under the ice he vowed he was not going to let the others die. He turned on his heel and ran back to the chapel. He picked up any loose stones he could find and made a great pile of them on the canal bank. All day he went to and fro, until he thought he had collected enough. Then he began to hurl them violently at the ice that first splintered and then began to crack and break up. By the time darkness began to fall he had opened up a twenty-foot strip of canal water for the kingfishers to dive into.

He was back the next morning after bolting his breakfast. He had expected to find it iced over once again. But although the edges of the ice had encroached somewhat, the water was still open to the sky. He found this difficult to understand for the night had been as cold as ever. He did not have to wait long for the explanation. He had been there no more than a few minutes when he heard a strange slapping slithery sound, and into view came a swan, still brown in her youth, staggering ungainly across the ice before letting herself gently into the

31

water. The neck was longer than he remembered and the grey had all but disappeared, but as she floated towards him now, the wings billowing like sails behind her, Billy had no doubt that this was indeed his swan come back to him.

'So, it was you swimming around that kept the ice back,' said Billy. 'Grown a bit, haven't you? Didn't recognise you at first. How's the wing then?' And as if to reply, the swan rose from the water and beat the air about her before settling back into the water again. 'Didn't break the ice for you, you know. Did it for them kingfishers, so don't you go frightening them off, will you now? They need to fish. Come to think of it, there can't be much about for you. Is that what you've come back for? Not just to see me. I can still speak—been able to ever since that day, and I've still got your feather you know. I'll get back home now and bring you some of Aunty May's stale crumpets—she never eats them. Don't know why she buys them. Don't go away.'

The swan stayed for a month or

more after that and by the end of that time was taking Aunty May's crumpets out of Billy's hand. He talked to her constantly and confessed for the first time what troubled him most—that he belonged nowhere, loved no one and was loved by no one. Once or twice she clambered out of the canal and allowed him to smooth the feathers on her neck. It was just as he was saying goodbye to her one evening, running his hand down the neck and over her folded wing feathers that he saw a large ring of red plastic around her left leg. 'Where'd you get that from?' he asked. 'You want to tell me, don't you? Funny, isn't it? I mean, you taught me to speak and you can't even speak yourself.'

Between them the boy and the swan kept open the pond on the canal for the kingfishers to feed, Billy breaking away the edges each morning to keep the ice back and the swan endlessly circling the water so that it was hardly ever still and could not freeze. No more kingfishers died and with Billy begging stale bread all over the estate no other bird in his Wilderness died of starvation that winter.

Then one night in March the frost lifted and the warm spring rain fell in torrents. When Billy arrived early the next morning he found the canal turned to water again. The swan was not there waiting for him as usual. He called out for her and ran up and down the bank, throwing bread into the water in a desperate attempt to bring her back. But all the while he knew she had gone. He felt suddenly deserted and rejected.

For some days he returned to wait for her, but she never came back. He found he could no longer be happy in his Wilderness without the swan. So he made up his mind to leave the Wilderness for ever, and he promised himself faithfully he would never return.

He kept his promise for a month or more, but then both boredom and a new yearning tempted him back. It was a bright day in a spring still chilled by a fresh north wind when Billy clambered back under the wire into his Wilderness. Already the skeletal trees were filling out with a new growth of leaves and the creeper was green again on the ruins. Billy ran across the graveyard to the canal, suddenly convinced that the swan would be there waiting for him as he had dreamed so often she would be. But the canal was deserted except for a moorhen that scooted into the reeds on the far bank. Seized with terrible despair he called out over the canal, 'Why don't you come back to me? Why? I saved you, didn't I? Didn't I save your life? I thought you were my friend. Please come back. Please.' But the whispering murmur of thousands of swarming starlings turned to a roar above his head and drowned his words.

Billy made his way back to the chapel and lay down out of the wind watching the clouds of starlings whirling in the sky over his Wilderness. He lay back on a mound in the middle of the chapel under the leaning lime tree and closed his eyes in an attempt to calm the anguish inside him, but all the misery welled up and he could not hold it back. He cried then as he had never cried before. The only hope, the only joy in his life had gone. All that was left for him was the thin-lipped Aunty May and the inhospitable hubbub of his school.

He must have cried himself to sleep for he was woken suddenly. He was lying on his side, his legs curled up so tight that his knees were touching his chin. At first he thought the sound might be the rustling of squirrels in the tree above him—he had seen them up there often enough before—but he had never heard squirrels yapping. Billy sat up. A blackbird piped at him from a blackthorn bush. Billy sat like a statue and waited. He allowed only his eyes to move and they scanned the trees above him, trained eyes now, keen and sharp. When it came again the sound was distant, yet it felt close, and it came not from the walls or the trees or the undergrowth around him, but from the ground beneath him, a curious squawking and squealing, almost bird-like, but no bird he knew could growl. He put an ear to the ground and listened. As he did so he noticed a strange musky smell in the grass. And from below the grass there was a dull yet distinct high-pitched yapping. Billy had heard enough and moved carefully off the mound, stepping slow and soft. He climbed over the stonework and settled down to watch, his heart beating in his ears.

One came out first, his white snub muzzle sniffing the air, and he was

butted out into the open by the one behind. And then two more emerged, almost together, until all four fox cubs stood like ridiculous infant sentinels, each one facing outwards, noses lifted, ears pricking and twitching. One of them was looking now at Billy but seemed not to see him. It was the largest of the cubs with a redder face than the others and more sharply defined black streaks running from the eyes to the muzzle. The eyes were grey and the nose that pointed at him earth brown. The fox cub sat down neatly and yawned, and Billy found himself

yawning in sympathy, a long yawn that lifted the shroud of despondency from Billy's shoulders and left him smiling and happy once again in his Wilderness.

CHAPTER FOUR

Billy looked on that day as they gambolled over the mound, stalking and pouncing on each other, rolling locked together down the slope and then springing apart again to play a remorseless game of tag and hide-and-seek. Then, as suddenly as it had begun it stopped, and a prolonged grooming session began, followed by a snooze in the thin spring sunlight—a bundle of foxes breathing as one. A crackling of twigs in the undergrowth was enough to awake them and send them scuttling down into the earth. Billy was about to leave, believing the show to be over, when he saw the vixen, a pigeon hanging from her mouth, padding through the graveyard, her white-tipped brush trailing behind her. He froze and prayed he had not been seen.

The cubs came out one by one to greet their mother and looked on patiently as the vixen neatly pulled away first the long grey primary feathers, then the downy secondaries until the pigeon was plucked clean. She kept shaking her head to rid her teeth of the feathers. The meal of regurgitated pigeon was soon over and each cub lay back replete while their mother checked them over in turn. And every few seconds she would lift her black nose and look about her nervously. She vanished down into the earth soon after the meal, taking her cubs with her. Billy was cold to the bone and he needed to stretch his cramped legs. He had seen enough for one day.

He crept away from the chapel as if every blade of grass might creak like a floorboard, and then he was outside the fence and hop-scotching successfully all the way home, never once allowing his feet to cross the cracks in the pavement. That night he took out his grey feather, held it in both hands, closed his eyes and willed the foxes to be there the next day. He knew that if the mother had caught his scent she might well take her cubs elsewhere. It was this dread that kept him awake most of that night.

He approached the den the next morning with the greatest caution, a damp forefinger in the air checking the wind direction to be sure they had no advance warning of his approach. But in his anxiety to see if they were still there he went too fast through the undergrowth, stumbled over a root and almost fell. Cursing himself silently he tiptoed on. He need not have worried, for the cubs lay in a pyramid on the mound just where they had been the day before, and Billy settled down to watch.

Each day during that first week of the spring holidays he came to the mound and sat behind the chapel wall to watch. After a week he could identify every fox cub, but his eye was always drawn to the largest of them, the boldest, the one that had looked at him that first day. This was the one that seemed to call the tune whenever the vixen was away hunting. The others went where he went. In any mock battles this one always ended up on top, astride his opponent and joyfully triumphant. This was the one that often stayed awake and on guard whilst the others slept, and Billy felt that only this fox cub was aware he was watching them, and he tolerated it because he understood that Billy was a benign presence that held no threat for them.

The vixen appeared to be hunting alone. If there was a dog fox helping her, Billy never saw him. The vixen was a splendid creature with a thick yellow-brown coat that bounced on her back as she moved. Billy admired her greatly, and not just for her looks. She worked tirelessly for her fox cubs. Every waking minute was devoted to their well-being. She was endlessly patient with them, supplying their every need, and seemingly spreading her affection and attention evenly between them. She brought back rabbits, mice, voles, minute shrews which the cubs threw into the air and juggled with; and judging by the variety of bones Billy found all over the mound, she must have visited every dustbin on the estate at one time or another in her endless struggle to keep her cubs alive.

On the Sunday before school began again for the summer term, Billy took a picnic lunch with him and spent the entire day fox-watching in the ruins. He wanted to make the best of his last day of freedom. He had not seen the vixen for a day or two and did not want to miss her. So he got there early and planned to stay until after dark. Aunty May would fret and fume, but he would risk that this time.

The fox cubs were much altered since he first saw them. It was as if their white muzzles had somehow been stretched, and pulled out to accommodate their teeth. Their noses were no longer brown but black. Conversely, their dark chocolate coats had turned to milk chocolate and the sparse wispy hair had been replaced by a thicker woolly pile.

They seemed unsettled when he arrived; only the larger one sat on top of the mound, his tail curled cat-like around his feet. The others yapped and whined anxiously around him, but he paid them little attention. They did not sleep much all that day either and their games were brief and ill-tempered; and much to Billy's disappointment they spent much of it underground. When they did appear, Billy noticed that one of them was listless, weak and unkempt. He felt something was wrong, but could not think what it was. He waited until it was dark for the vixen to appear, but again she did not. The cubs had gone below and were silent. Billy put his ear to the ground and listened. He could hear nothing. He left them to make his way home for supper.

He found a crowd gathered under the amber glow of the light outside the flats. Billy had to shield his eyes against the glaring headlights of a car as he ran towards it. Everyone was there—Aunty May running out in her fluffy mauve slippers and her curlers—and all the children were there in their dressing-gowns. But the crowd was strangely silent. As Billy pushed his way through he already knew what he would find. The vixen lay in the gutter, tongue lolling out, her unseeing eyes glinting fluorescent orange under the light. She was matted and muddied, and somehow smaller in death.

'I tried to stop—thought it was a dog,' said the man who was kneeling over her. 'Just staggered out in front of me, she did, almost as if she wanted me to hit her. Looked to me as if she'd been hit once already—either that or she was drunk. She was dragging her back legs. I just finished her off. That's all. Not my fault. Only a fox anyway. Don't belong to anyone, does it?' So many feelings were racing through Billy's mind; grief at the vixen's death, anger at its cause, and anxiety for the fox cubs left hungry in the Wilderness.

Everyone of course had to have their look. Someone wanted to cut off the brush for a trophy, but it was agreed in the end that the fox should be dumped in the dustbin for collection in the morning, before it began to smell. Billy made sure which dustbin it was before Aunty May took his hand and hauled him away. 'I've been waiting for you for nearly two hours, Billy,' she said. 'Could have been you run over out

47

there. I've told you time and again to get back home before dark. Worried sick I was. You got school tomorrow and you haven't had a bath for days; and look at you, Billy, you're filthy again. What do you get up to? No point in asking, I know. You never say anything, do you Billy? It's not fair, Billy. It's not fair at all.'

Billy stole out of the flat before first light, taking the trowel Aunty May used for her flower boxes and ran down to the dustbin. The vixen lay curled up at the bottom of the dustbin. Were it not for her unnatural stillness she could have been asleep. Billy cradled her in his arms, and keeping away from the street lights ran across the estate towards the Wilderness. The vixen was heavy, heavier than he had imagined, and he had to stop and put her down several times before he reached the fence. The Wilderness was alive with birdsong.

He removed the turf carefully. The earth was soft in the graveyard and within half an hour he had dug deep enough. He prepared a smooth earth bed and laid the vixen gently to rest. He hated to cover her up, but once he had begun the job he wanted to finish it and was quick about it. He laid the turfs back over the earth and trod them down with his foot. He stood for a moment looking down at the grave. 'I'll look after them for you,' he said. 'Don't you worry. I promise I'll look after them.'

He found a small branch that had fallen from the lime tree and pulled off the twigs until he was left with a cross. He pushed it firmly into the ground, picked a few primroses from the ruins and covered the grave with them. Then he turned away and left her there.

Inside the walls of the ruined chapel nothing stirred. Billy knelt down at the mouth of the den and spoke in a whisper. 'It's all right,' he said. 'It's Billy, Billy Bunch. I'm your mother now, d'you hear me, and I'm going to be looking after you. Be back at lunch time with some food. You'll be all right. You'll see.' And he ran down to the canal and washed the earth off the trowel.

Had he looked up then he
have seen the swan watching
motionless in the black water. B
did not.

He turned and made for home. The
street lights were still on as he raced
across the estate. He had the presence
of mind, before he climbed into bed, to
take a tin of dried milk and two tins of
corned beef from the larder and push
them down to the bottom of his duffle
bag. The rest he thought he would save
back from his school dinner as he had
done last winter for the birds.

At school they had an hour's break
for dinner. He usually ate alone if he
could find an empty table, and he
managed that today, so it was nothing
to slip the beefburgers and treacle tart
into his duffle bag, and nothing to hide
away the two blue plastic bowls. He ran
out of the playground and made for the
Wilderness. The mound was deserted
when he arrived and that suited him.
He did not want to frighten them away
before they had a chance to get to
know him. He opened the corned beef
and emptied it out in four separate

51

piles, making a trail of corned beef crumbs right to the mouth of the den. He broke the beefburgers in half and put each half onto the piles of corned beef. The treacle tart had disintegrated in the bottom of his duffle bag, but he gathered the sticky bits to garnish each cub's meal. The two plastic bowls he filled with water from the canal and then slowly sprinkled on the milk powder and stirred it with his finger until it became thick and creamy. Then he retreated behind his wall to wait. He heard the school bell go for the end of playtime. If he did not go now, he knew he would be missed, and that would mean trouble; but he could not bring himself to leave. He had to be sure they would take the food—he certainly didn't want anything else to take it. The noise from the distant playground faded and he was left in the sudden silence of the Wilderness.

As he expected, the largest of them came out first. Hesitant and uncertain he sniffed at the corned beef, backed away from it, sat down and ignored it studiously, surveying all around for some minutes before he decided it was safe to try a taste of it. A short yap of command brought the other three tumbling into the open and they attacked one pile together, all four of them, before moving on to the next. It was not as Billy had planned it but he was delighted none the less. They found the milk and lapped both bowls clean. When he was sure they had had their fill he rose up slowly from behind the wall so that they could see him. All four stayed for just a moment by the bowls, looking up at him and licking their lips, before three of them dashed into the den, leaving only the biggest of them behind.

The boy and the fox cub looked at each other in silence for a full minute. Neither moved a muscle. Then the fox turned and walked away. At the mouth of the den he stopped to consider Billy again, sat down to scratch himself and then disappeared into the earth.

CHAPTER FIVE

Billy was so overjoyed at his success that he quite forgot to prepare himself for the onslaught that was awaiting him at home. Aunty May was at him before he could close the door behind him. 'I want to know where you've been, Billy,' she said, her thin lips quivering with rage. Billy looked up at her and felt sorry for her. 'Mr Brownlow from the school rang me after lunch and told me you had vanished—just not come back, he said—and I've been worried sick ever since, sick, Billy. How could you do this to me? Five foster children I've had and not one of them ever played truant, not one, until you. And both my own boys never missed a day of school, not one day. It's too bad, Billy, too bad.' She was near to tears and Billy liked her at that moment for the first time. Then she spoilt it by following up with the usual threat: 'Now if you don't tell me Billy, right now, where you've been all afternoon, you know what will

happen, don't you?'

   'Been out,' said Billy.

   'Where?'

   'Dunno, just out. Didn't feel well, did I? Came on all dizzy like.'

'Then why didn't you come home, Billy?'

'Dunno. Couldn't find the way, could I? Dizzy, wasn't I?'

It was all on the spur of the moment, a lie that was wafer thin and Billy knew it; but as it turned out it was the very best story he could have dreamed up. If he'd had an entire week to make up the story it could not have been better.

Within the hour he was inside the doctor's surgery and explaining the symptoms in more detail. The doctor, who had tufts of red hair growing out of his ears, pressed and prodded him all over, and Aunty May kept muttering that she'd always fed him right and that no child of hers had ever had this trouble before. In the end the doctor diagnosed a mild infection of the middle ear, gave him some antibiotic and said he should come back in a week if it wasn't better.

'What about school, Doctor?' Aunty May asked, dragging Billy to the door by his wrist.

'No school,' said the doctor, without looking up. 'Up and about at home, but no school. And best to wrap up warm when he goes out. And he should go out. Fresh air is good for all of us. Don't coop him up.'

Billy could not believe his good fortune as he walked home that evening with Aunty May. She was going on about how she knew all along there must be something wrong with him to go wandering off from school like that, and how Mr Brownlow had no right to accuse one of her boys of playing truant. 'Teachers these days,' she said, shaking her head. 'They're just too young, like the policemen. It's what I've always said—no experience. You need experience to look after children—and you have to be sensitive. That Mr Brownlow wouldn't know it if he stepped on a hedgehog with his bare feet. Now Billy, dear, we're going to have to feed you up and get you strong again, aren't we?'

So long as Billy was smothered in at least two scarves, a coat and a Balaclava, Aunty May let him go out for long walks on his own, but he had to be back for meal times. Billy mentioned as casually as he could that his favourite food these days was corned beef hash. Of course he detested it, but it had the desired result. Aunty May went out and bought two dozen tins of it—it was cheaper that way—to join the others on the shelf in the larder. Billy thought that he could keep his foxes alive on about two tins of corned beef a day, washed down with milk. And it was not difficult under all his protective clothing to disguise the fact that he was carrying two tins of corned beef each morning when he went out and a plastic bag of milk powder. Aunty May did not seem to notice that the pile of corned beef tins at the back of the larder was diminishing rather too quickly, but just in case she did, Billy made a point of making himself occasional corned beef sandwiches which he forced himself to eat in front of her. And she never even looked in the old tin of milk powder. When it ran out after a few days, Billy spent all his sweet money on replacing it.

Fortunately the fox cubs never

seemed to tire of their new diet and came out for it whenever they heard Billy coming through the Wilderness. They would be waiting for him on the mound and although they still kept their distance as he opened the tins and spooned it out onto the grass, they were coming closer to him each day. Billy was often tempted to reach out and touch them as they fed, but he felt that would be a risk, and perhaps a liberty this soon. They would come to him and want to be touched only when they trusted him completely. He would wait.

He would sit cross-legged on the mound, and the fox cubs would play around him now, for the most part ignoring him completely; but occasionally they would all four sit and look at him. He thought he ought to speak to them then, but decided words might be too sharp. So he would hum gently and when they became used to this he would put words to the tunes— his own words and his own tunes. And they listened, ears pricked, heads on one side, fascinated—for a time. But there were always interruptions to spoil his brief concerts—a tempting tail to pounce on, an essential scratch behind the ear, a dead leaf that just had to be chased. As Billy expected, it was always the largest cub that was his most loyal listener, his grey eyes never leaving Billy's face as he sang.

This fox was the first to take food

from Billy's hand some days later. He was the first to submit to being touched, and once he had consented the others followed almost at once. Now they would play, not just around Billy as he sat on the mound, but with him. They sprang over his legs, hid behind his back, chewed on his shoes and lay up against him to sleep. He had their trust now, and their love. He had kept his promise to the dead vixen.

The absence of the swan was all that saddened him. Every day after he had covered the vixen's grave with fresh flowers he would make his way through the graveyard to the canal just in case

she should be there waiting for him. He was no longer offended that she wasn't there. Curiously, he felt quite certain that he would see her again one day. Meanwhile he had his foxes to care for, and they needed him.

He stayed with them now every minute he could, only returning home for the obligatory meals and the inevitable questions from Aunty May that he fended off with increasing skill.

All this time Aunty May suspected nothing. When asked where he had been Billy would always just reply, 'Out'. Only once was his secret nearly discovered, and then it was the foxes' fault and not his. It was the musky smell of the foxes that Billy brought home with him on his clothes that nearly gave the game away with Aunty May. As he came into the flat one evening, she wrinkled her nose up and insisted on knowing where he had been and what he had been up to. Billy parried the questions as best he could. 'Then you been rolling in something, Billy,' she said.

'No, Aunty May,' he said. 'Don't

think I have.'

'Well you smell something rotten,' she said. 'And don't you come sitting on my good sitting-room furniture smelling like that. I don't know what you get up to Billy, I really don't. Sometimes I think I'd be better off without you, I really do. Now get those stinking clothes off. I'll have to wash them again.'

After feigning another dizzy spell one evening as he got up from the kitchen table after tea, Billy managed to extend the doctor's diagnosis of his middle ear infection for three more wonderful weeks. By this time, though, the cubs' appetites seemed to have doubled. They always seemed hungry now, even after their meals, and Billy realised he was not going to be able to supply their food only from Aunty May's larder for much longer without arousing suspicion. 'I know you love it, Billy,' Aunty May had said on more than one occasion, 'but I must be buying in at least a dozen tins a week of that corned beef. Can't think where you put it all. Eat me out of house and home you will.'

Suddenly, much to Aunty May's relief, his dizzy spells ceased, and he returned to school where he had to endure Mr Brownlow's inevitably sarcastic welcome. Billy had his reasons for going back. He knew that there were always vast quantities of left-overs after school dinners and they had to be put somewhere. He determined to find out where that was. His investigations led him to a row of black dustbins outside the kitchen door behind the school. They were conventionally hidden round the corner and not overlooked by any windows, and he was able to rifle through the dustbins with little chance of being discovered. There was enough there to feed an army of foxes, but he chose only what he thought the fox cubs would appreciate most—sausages, bread rolls and cheese.

As it turned out he chose badly, for when he emptied his duffle bag on the mound that afternoon during lunch break, the fox cubs simply played with the sausages, tossing them into the air and ignored the rest. He tried to encourage them by breaking the sausages open, but although they ate some of the cheese they were still unenthusiastic. 'What's the matter with you?' he said. 'I can't get you corned beef all the time. They don't serve it up at school—no one would touch it if they did. Look, I know it's school food, but it's food isn't it? It's not that bad.' But the foxes clearly did not agree and they lay down together in a disconsolate, disappointed pile. 'All right,' said Billy, 'I'll see if I can find something better, but it won't be until after teatime.' They would not play with him that day, so he left them and made his way unhappily back to school. He would have to raid the dustbins once again, he thought. There was nothing else to be done.

Billy was sitting alone on the steps of the mobile classroom waiting for afternoon lessons to begin and wondering how he could lay his hands on a large supply of corned beef without having to shop-lift it when there was a scream of delight from the direction of the school gates. He ignored it at first, but then sauntered over to see what was up. The playground fence was lined from end to end with children, noses pressed through the mesh and clinging on with their fingers; and there was a rush of running children all about him and the teacher's strident voice above his head. 'What's the matter here?'

' 'S'a fox, sir,' said someone.

'Foxes. There's three of 'em,' said someone else. Billy barged his way to the front of the crowd.

'Well I never, bold as brass,' said the teacher, standing beside him. 'Never seen that before, have you, Billy?'

'No, sir,' said Billy quickly. 'Never.'

Three fox cubs were sitting out on the grass in the open just outside the fence. The children cooed with delight, but the *oohs* and *aahs* were soon superceded by a vociferous band of hunters that aimed their fingers through the wire and blasted away at the fox cubs, who, suddenly alarmed by the distant hullabaloo, wriggled back under the wire and vanished into the

66

undergrowth of the Wilderness beyond.

That afternoon Mr Brownlow made them write a story about foxes, but Billy could not write a word. He sat stunned by his window, and when Mr Brownlow asked why he had not written anything he said he wasn't feeling too well. And this time it was no lie.

CHAPTER SIX

That afternoon after school, Billy ran home and took three tins of corned beef off the shelf and just hoped he'd be able to replace them before Aunty May noticed. He took particular care no one was watching him when he crawled under the wire into the Wilderness. The fox cubs were ravenous, snarling and snapping at each other as they waited for the tins to be opened, and then they attacked the corned beef voraciously. When they had finished not a shred was left on the grass. In their anxiety to drink the milk, they stood on the edges of the bowls and upset them, sending the milk soaking into the ground. Twice more he had to fill them up from the canal and mix up the milk powder before they were satisfied. Then when Billy lay down they spread themselves all over him and cleaned themselves, each other and Billy, minutely.

'You sillies,' said Billy. 'Why did you

have to come out and show yourselves like that? I'd have brought the food. I'd have found it somewhere. I told you didn't I? Have I ever let you down yet? Well, have I? Now they know where you are and I got to move you. That's what your mother would do but I don't know where I can move you to. There's nowhere else round here for foxes 'cept the Wilderness. Can't hardly take you home, can I? You must never, never come out again. They're nasty out there, d'you understand, nasty. They'd shoot you soon as look at you.' One of them, the one with the whitest muzzle, sat down on his face as if to stop him talking. 'I'm beginning to think Aunty May's right, you know. You do smell something rotten. Can't see how 'cos you wash yourselves every five minutes. Still 'spect you think I smell pretty funny. Wonder what we do smell like, people I mean?'

He stayed longer than ever that evening. He didn't want to leave them alone at all; and when he did have to leave them at last he turned to give them a final warning, wagging his finger at them. 'You 'member what I said, now,' he said. 'Stay here. Stay here and be good and I'll be back tomorrow sometime. Corned beef, I promise. Dunno how, but corned beef it will be. But don't you move out of the Wilderness, you understand?' But the fox cubs were all busy washing themselves and hardly gave him a glance as he left them.

Billy could not sleep that night. He lay on his back, hands under his head, and tried to think, but his thoughts were forever being interrupted by the rumble and roar of traffic from the motorway, by yowling cats, or by Aunty May turning over in her squeaking bed and coughing her dry smoker's cough. It was the first warm night of the summer, and Billy discarded his blankets one by one until he was left only with his sheet. Even then he could not sleep. By morning he had still not worked out how he was going to find enough corned beef to feed his foxes; neither had he managed to think of a place where it would be safe enough to hide the cubs. But move them he knew he must, and quickly.

He survived school that day only because Aunty May had unwittingly solved the problem of the corned beef for him. At breakfast she handed over his dinner money for the week. It wouldn't be stealing, he thought, as he joined the cavalcade of children walking to school. It wasn't as if he was taking from her any more than usual. He would spend it all on corned beef and go without school dinners for the week—just tell them at school that he would be going home for dinner. No one would know. Lots of children did it, after all.

Throughout the dinner break there was a line of fox-watchers by the school fence, binoculars at the ready. But when after an hour nothing appeared, they soon gave up. By the time the bell went for afternoon lessons Billy found he was one of only a few left at the fence and he did not for one moment take his eye from the spot where the foxes had appeared the day before. He longed to run over to the Wilderness, crawl under the wire and be with them, to reassure them. More than once he thought he spotted some unnatural movement in the undergrowth beyond the wire and held his breath, fully expecting them to come out into the open. Forehead pressed against the school fence, he willed them to stay hidden, and they did.

The appearance of the fox cubs was still the buzz of the school. There was talk of clandestine expeditions into the Wilderness to find them, talk of setting the dogs upon them. This only served to convince Billy that he had to act fast if he was to save them. By the time school finished that afternoon he still did not know what could be done. On the way home for tea he stopped at the shops to buy as much corned beef as his dinner money would allow. That problem at any rate he had solved, at least for the time being.

He was into his second helping of baked beans and had scraped away all the beans off the toast as he always did, when Aunty May took the cigarette out of her lips, took the cosy off the teapot and poured herself a cup of tea. She sat down opposite him and flicked the ash off her cigarette into the ashtray. 'Did you hear about those fox cubs, Billy?' she asked suddenly, but she did not wait for an answer. 'Four of them there was—that's what my friend Ivy told me, you know Ivy at number 38—and she

said Mrs Bootle told her and she's on the Committee so she ought to know, shouldn't she? Well, someone spotted one of them a few days ago just down by that old ruin, just outside the fence it was. You know the place, Billy? Then yesterday there was three of them seen from the school. Children came home full of it, Ivy said. You didn't see them, Billy, did you? Don't suppose you did—didn't say anything about it, did you? Well anyway Mrs Bootle wasn't going to have it. Vermin are vermin, like she says, and when they grow up they only breed, don't they? And they're into dustbins all the time, spreading litter and disease. And Ivy says she knows her tabby cat was eaten by a fox last year—couldn't have been anything else, she says. And like Mrs Bootle says, they're a danger to health. I mean did you smell that dead fox a few weeks back? And she says they've been known to attack children in their prams when they're hungry enough. And they don't wash, you know, they don't ever wash. Well they wouldn't, would they? Anyway, Mrs Bootle, she's

Chairman of the Committee now, you know, well she wasn't having it, like I said. She rang up the Pest Control people last night and they came quick as lightning first thing this morning. Not surprising really—been a lot of complaints about vermin on the estate. What's the matter, Billy? Don't you like your baked beans? Told me you could eat like a horse. Something the matter with you? You eat up, there's a good boy. Like I was saying, they went in and gassed them, just like that. Good thing too, I should say. Met Mrs Cole at the supermarket and her husband that works on the Council, he was there—he was one of them that did it. You won't ever go near that place, will you, Billy? Mrs Cole told me, she said there's been strange goings-on in there—you know, like rituals, witches and that. She said they found a cross of twigs stuck into the ground and a fresh grave with flowers on it. Don't you ever go near that place, Billy, do you hear? Come on now Billy, eat your baked beans. I opened a big tin and you said you'd eat it. It's not right to waste things, Billy, I'm not made of money you know.'

'How many did you say they found?' Billy asked, blinking back the tears that threatened to engulf him, wiping them away from the corners of his eyes.

'One cross is quite enough, Billy,' she said, stubbing out her cigarette. 'People get up to all sorts in places like that, Black Magic, Voodoo. You keep away, like I said.'

'Foxes,' said Billy patiently. 'How many foxes did they find?'

'Oh, I don't know. Think it was four. Do wish you'd stop playing with those beans and eat up, Billy. They'll be all cold if you leave them much longer. No, perhaps it was three they killed. Maybe it was four, I don't know. Three, four, what's the difference? Anyway, Mrs Cole said they'd be going back in to flush out any more if there are any. Are you crying, Billy? Are you all right, dear? Oh Billy, there's no need for that. You don't have to eat the baked beans if you don't want to. I can keep them back for tomorrow. There's no need to cry, Billy.' Billy wept silently, his tears falling from his cheeks onto the baked beans. 'All this fuss over beans, Billy,' said Aunty May. 'I've never known you cry before, and now this and all because of baked beans. You'll spoil them, Billy. I don't understand you at all, Billy, I've never understood you. I don't like to see boys who cry, Billy. You're a big boy now. Crying's for babies, Billy, not big boys. You go and lie on your bed till you feel better, there's a good boy.'

Billy threw himself face down onto his bed and buried his face in his pillow. He had to bite on his knuckles to hold back the scream of anguish that threatened to burst from him. He was consumed with a terrible grief at the loss of his family, and a raging anger at the ignorance and cruelty that had killed them. As he lay there he could find only one vestige of hope remaining, the possibility that there could be one of them still left alive. Aunty May had not been sure whether it was three or four. He clung desperately to that hope, took his grey feather out from under his pillow and willed it to be three. When Aunty May came in later on he pretended to be asleep; breathing deeply as she covered him with the blanket. He waited until she had gone to bed and the light in the passage had been switched off before slipping out of the flat.

It was one of those rare summer nights when the white light of the moon was strong enough to all but eliminate the omnipotent glare of the street lamps. Billy ran down across the estate towards the Wilderness, his grey feather in his pocket. He ran all the way there, half hoping, half dreading what he would find. Once in the Wilderness he moved silently through the graveyard and into the ruined chapel itself. The sound of his own panting filled the ruins as he sat down on the mound and waited.

There was destruction all around him. All the entrances to the den had been caved in, and great mounds of fresh earth covered each one. He put his ear to the ground and listened. He could hear nothing but his own heartbeat and his own frantic

78

breathing. He lay there for some time, hoping and praying that one of them might have survived the gassing, but as time passed and he heard nothing he feared the worst, but refused to believe it. It took several minutes of frantic digging to clear away enough earth from one of the holes so that he could call down into the den. 'It's me. It's Billy. You can come out now. It's me. It's Billy.' But there was no answering movement from inside the earth, no sound at all.

Time after time Billy's hopes were raised, only to be dashed again. There was a sudden rustling in the undergrowth that turned out to be a small hedgehog shuffling through the leaves, then a noisy commotion on the canal when something alarmed the ducks and sent them quacking into the air. Billy reached the canal in time to see a big fish jump—a marauding pike, he thought. Billy searched his Wilderness from end to end. He called down every rabbit hole; he even climbed the walls of the ruined chapel to check any window-ledge where a fox

might be lying up. It was all for nothing.

Towards dawn he found himself wandering disconsolately towards the canal bank where he sat down and at last accepted that all his foxes had been taken from him, that none of them had survived. The great white moon shone up at him from the water and he threw a stone at it angrily to stop it staring at him. It shattered into a million jewels before piecing itself together once again. He had no tears left now. Exhausted and drained of all care, Billy lay down and slept.

The swan came out of the reeds, gliding across the water, and looked on as the boy slept. In his sleep Billy dreamed she was there and he smiled.

CHAPTER SEVEN

A cold nose in his ear tried to drag him from his dreams. He was dreaming that the swan had brought the foxes to him, and he did not want the dream to end, for he knew he was dreaming and that nothing now could bring them to him. He did not want to be interrupted and so he pushed the cold nose away. But the nose would not be denied and nudged him awake. Billy opened his eyes. The fox sat beside him, his tail curled round his feet, looking down at him. Billy still revelled in his dream. It was only when the fox yawned and came to lie down beside him, laying his head on his arm that Billy began to understand that he was living his dream, and that his dream was not a dream at all. Billy sat up at once and looked at the canal to see if the other part of his dream was true; but there was no swan, only the white moon still staring at him from the water. 'You're the only one, then?' said Billy looking

around him. 'You're the only one that got away, and I bet I know which one you are. You're the biggest one, aren't you? You heard them coming, didn't you? Knew it wasn't me, didn't you? Bet you told the others to follow you and they didn't. Where you been hiding all this time?' The fox seemed to welcome his caresses, rolling on to his back as Billy's hand ran through his fur. The fur was wet to the touch. 'Not raining is it? Oh, so that's it. You swam the canal, didn't you? No other way you could have got wet all over like this is there? Foxed them, didn't you? Foxed them good and proper. Now I've got to get you out of here. Aunty May said they'd be back. Can't leave you here. There's nowhere else to go but home. I'll work something out, don't know what, but something.' He knelt up and put his arms around the fox and hugged him close. 'I'm never going to let them get you. Never. But you'll have to do as I tell you. First you'll have to walk on a lead, so that I can get you home. You got to learn, and learn fast. Only got my belt. It's a bit short but it'll have to do.'

Billy slipped the belt over the fox's head, pulled it tight so that it fitted snugly around his neck, and then gently lifted the fox to his feet. There was some resistance at first, a shaking of the head, a few attempts to gnaw at the belt, but a turn or two around the graveyard and the fox seemed happy to be led, just so long as Billy did not jerk the lead too sharply. As they passed the vixen's grave, Billy wanted to tell her what had happened but he could not find the words. He had let her down and he could not bring himself to confess it.

The estate was just waking up when Billy came out of the Wilderness with the fox. The milk float was humming through the streets and the lights were on in the paper shop on the corner. The only car he saw was a police car cruising slowly around the estate. Billy dared not run too fast for fear of pulling too hard on the lead and upsetting the fox; so he trotted gently, keeping the lead slack. Every few paces though, the fox would stop and look about him. Billy had to talk him on, calming his fears, stroking his head and ears until he was happy to go on again.

The journey seemed interminably long to Billy, but they reached the door to the flats without being spotted. Nothing would persuade the fox to follow Billy through the doors no matter how hard Billy tried to make him. In the end he was forced to pick him up and climb the echoing stairway to the tenth floor. Aunty May never woke up until the alarm went at eight, so he felt quite safe as he stole into the flat and closed the front door behind him. But even as he put his hand onto his bedroom door to push it open, he felt someone watching him from the kitchen.

The light went on and Aunty May was there, standing by the kitchen table, her face pasty white and drawn without its make-up. Billy kept his back to her, one arm holding the fox tightly to his chest. 'Billy, Billy,' Aunty May was crying; Billy was not sure if she was crying with fury or with relief. 'Where've you been, Billy? All night

I've been up, all night. The police are out looking for you, have been ever since midnight, when I found your bed empty. Now what am I going to say to them, Billy? It's too much, Billy, too much.' She came towards him, gathering her dressing-gown around her. 'What's that you're hiding there, Billy? Show me, show me at once.' And she took Billy by the shoulder and swung him round to face her. Billy expected her to scream but she did not. Her mouth gaped in horror as she backed away from him, knocking over the kitchen stool behind her. 'Get that thing out of here,' she whispered. 'Get it out. Billy, either you put that thing out of that door this minute or . . . or . . . Billy, either it goes at once, or you both go. Do you understand me, Billy? Do you understand what I'm saying?'

'Yes, Aunty May,' said Billy. And with the fox cradled against him he walked to the front door and opened it. 'Goodbye,' he said, and he was gone before she could collect herself.

Billy ran towards the canal, the only way he could go. The estate lay in a triangle of two main roads with the canal behind. The roads led only into the city and there was no refuge there for a boy and a fox on the run. Billy had often looked out across the canal and seen the hills rising into the clouds on the horizon, and common sense told him that this was where he had to go. There were scarcely any houses on those high hills, and that meant fewer people. It was the countryside, an empty place where people went for picnics in the summer time and where he had always longed to go. Billy had seen it fleetingly, flashing by out of coach windows, but he had never been there. It seemed to him the kind of place a boy and a fox could lose themselves and never be found. As Billy ran across the estate, the fox trotting out alongside him, he could hear Aunty May calling out after him to come back. It only made him run faster.

Quite how he planned to cross the canal Billy did not know, and he had not had the time to think about it. Even as he stood now, looking out across the weed-choked water to the far bank, he still had no idea how he would get across, for Billy could not swim. He could splash and kick enough to keep himself afloat for a few brief seconds in the shallow end of the pool in swimming lessons, but then panic invariably overtook him and his legs would reach for the bottom. It had been different when he rescued the swan. Then he had had no time to think about it. The fox stood beside him panting hard, glad of the rest. 'All right, so you can swim,' said Billy. 'Comes natural to a fox I suppose. Nearest bridge over the canal is the main road and they'd catch us before we got there. No choice, have we?' He remembered then that he had not drowned the last time he jumped in. He remembered he had felt the mud under his feet and he had managed to keep his head above the water. That memory and the sight of Aunty May bearing down on him, dressing-gown flying out behind her, screaming out for him to stop, was all the spur Billy needed. He pushed the fox out into the canal and watched him paddle away before jumping in after him.

He sank at once, his feet kicking out desperately for the bottom, which did not seem to be there as he had expected. He came up again gasping for air and flailing the water to keep himself afloat. Ahead of him he could see the fox's white muzzle nosing through the weeds and he struck out after him, legs and arms working frantically in an untidy dog paddle. But the far bank came no closer and he was tiring fast. He pounded the water furiously, but no matter how hard he tried he seemed unable to prevent his body from sinking. By the time he reached the middle of the canal he had swallowed a lot of water and was choking. The weeds were wrapping around his legs and dragging him down. He could see that the fox had reached the bank safely and was shaking himself, and that gave him new heart, but his legs seemed incapable now of obeying him. He knew then that he was going to drown, that there was nothing he could do about it, no point in struggling any more.

He had sunk twice already when he saw a branch floating slowly towards him and reached out for it. He caught at the twigs and hauled it towards him until he could cling to the branch itself. He hooked his arms over it and kicked his legs free of the weed, and as he did so he found he was moving slowly towards the fox on the bank. So he kept kicking and kicking until the branch edged its way into the reeds and would go no further. Billy threw himself down on the bank by the fox and coughed the water out of his lungs.

Only the fox saw the swan glide away, in under the shadow of the hanging alder trees, and he stiffened momentarily with surprise.

Billy looked up to find Aunty May standing on the bank opposite. 'Now you come back here this minute, Billy Bunch,' she shouted. 'This minute, d'you hear?' Billy said nothing, but walked away through the long grass, the fox at his heels. 'Well good riddance then, Billy Bunch,' she screamed. 'There's plenty more where

you come from, always will be. Don't
think you can come running back to me
when they pick you up either. I won't
have you, you hear? I won't have you.
You take your filthy fox and run for all
I care. P'raps that's where you belong,
Billy Bunch, out there in the wild with

the animals, with that fox.' But Billy
was out of earshot by now and running
and leaping through the grass, his eyes
on the thin grey line of light that was
creeping up over the dark and distant
hills.

Those hills beckoned him all
morning as he trudged on through the
grass-waving meadows and across the
sun-spangled streams, but they seemed
to come no nearer. Often in the valleys
he would lose sight of the hills
completely and become swallowed up

in the immensity of the countryside; and when the hills did reappear there always seemed to be villages or farmyards in the way, between him and the hills, places where he knew there would be people, places he knew they had to avoid. That the police would be looking for them all over the countryside Billy had no doubt; and he could not doubt that they already knew in which direction he had gone. They would know well enough where to look for them. If he were to be sighted now it would be the end of everything. They would take his fox away from him and he would never see him again. With that terrible threat hanging over him he moved only under cover, as far as possible keeping to the hedgerows and the woods. If that meant going the long way round, then he went the long way round.

Only once that morning did he stray too near a farmhouse. He was not to know that the smell of the fox would carry on the wind and draw the sheepdog towards them. They were making their way stealthily across a farm track and then into a cut hayfield the other side when the sheepdog came at them suddenly, hackles up, its body stiff with fury at them. The fox jerked away violently, snapping the lead, and bolted into the hedgerow. Billy's instinct too was to run, but the dog was too close and he knew he could not run fast enough. So he stood his ground, his spine warm with fear, and faced the hysterical barking and the bared teeth. When it went for his ankles he lashed out viciously, landing a lucky kick on its side that sent it scampering away, tail tucked abjectly between its legs. It took several minutes of patient persuasion for him to cajole the fox out from the sanctuary of the hedge.

Billy had nothing to use for a lead now and wondered if the fox would follow him up the track. Walking backwards, he whistled him up and called him. At first the fox sat watching him in the middle of the track, head on one side, thinking. Billy kept walking and whistled again. Whether the fox grasped the idea or whether he just did not want to be left alone there Billy did not know, but the fox came loping up the lane after him. After that he seemed not to want to stray more than a few paces from Billy's feet, and if he ever did Billy's whistle would always bring him back.

CHAPTER EIGHT

As the day wore on, the sun beat relentlessly down on their backs. Billy was glad of it, for it dried his soaking clothes as he walked; but with only stream water inside them both boy and fox began to weaken. As he tired, Billy began to take more risks, and in his anxiety to get as far as possible from the city before nightfall he became careless. Where before he had kept close to the edges of fields, hugging the hedgerows, now he would take the shortest route, walking openly out across fields where they might be seen from the farmhouses. He knew well enough that they were more exposed to discovery on the roads than anywhere else. Until now he had been scrupulously careful to ensure there was no one about, no traffic approaching, before crossing; and he had always picked up the fox and carried him across. But when in the late afternoon they came to a narrow, winding lane he did not even bother to pick up the fox and gave only a cursory glance down the lane. He was about half-way across, and whistling for the fox to follow him, when the little girl on the bicycle came round the bend fast. She skidded to a halt on the gravelly

road, using her feet for brakes.

'Didn't see you,' she said. 'Haven't got no brakes—busted.' As she spoke, the fox walked nonchalantly out across the road towards Billy, belatedly obeying his call. 'Hey, isn't that a fox?' she said.

'No, it isn't,' said Billy.

'He is,' she said. 'I seen 'em in books, and my dad shot one once when it

came around the fowls. 'S a fox, that is, 's a fox.'

'Just looks like a fox,' said Billy. ' 'T'isn't really.' The girl, he thought, was a little younger than he was, with long blond pigtails and an open smiling face, the kind, Billy thought, that would talk a lot. He would have to be convincing. 'Looks like a fox, I know,' he said. 'Everyone says so, but it's just a funny kind of sheepdog—still a puppy he is really. I mean you've never heard of a fox you could stroke, have you? I mean they're wild animals, foxes are. Like wolves they are, sort of, take your hand off they would, give 'em half a chance.' And he crouched down and stroked the fox's neck, burying his fingers in the soft fur. 'Good dog,' he said. 'Good dog. See? Quiet as a mouse, he is. No need to be frightened of him. He won't hurt you. Wouldn't hurt a fly, would you, boy? Come on, you have a go.' The girl stepped off her bike and laid it down in the middle of the road.

'You sure he's all right?' she said, approaching nervously. The fox sat quite still, looking up at Billy for reassurance. Billy felt his whole body stiffen as the girl touched him, and when his ears went back on his head Billy feared he might be betrayed, but as the girl relaxed, her petting became less tentative and she was soon smoothing him all over and enjoying it. 'Never seen a dog like this before,' she said. ' 'Spose it'll look proper when it's grown up.'

' 'Spose so,' said Billy, much relieved at the success of his ruse but conscious of the fact that a car could come down the road at any moment and that the driver might not be so gullible as this girl. 'You'd better pick your bike up before someone comes round that bend. Got to be going now.' And he opened the field gate and whistled for the fox to come after him, and then walked away out into the field as casually as he could.

'Where you going?' called the girl, following him to the gate.

'Home,' said Billy, waving his hand above his head.

'Where's that?' she cried. But Billy

101

pretended he had not heard and walked on a little faster, not so fast that it could be thought he was running away, but fast enough to get away from her questions. 'My dad's a farmer and he says you should ought to keep dogs on the lead, they'll end up chasing sheep else. And you ought to shut gates, don't you know that?' On the brow of the hill Billy looked back over his shoulder to be sure he was not being followed and she was gone. He broke into a run, cursing himself aloud for his carelessness.

After that, exhausted as he was, he took no more risks. He had had his warning and did not ignore it. As evening came on his stomach began to ache with hunger and he could think of little else but food. He thought of raiding vegetable gardens, of stealing eggs and even of venturing into a village under the cover of darkness to rifle the dustbins. But the dread of capture was stronger even than the nagging hunger pains that tugged at his stomach.

He found talking helped him to

forget, providing he could avoid the subject of food, but somehow it always came back to that. By nightfall they still had had nothing to eat. The last red of the sun bled into the clouds above the glowing city in the distance. Billy sat with his fox on the bracken hillside. 'Looks pretty from here,' he said. 'But we're never going back there. You and me, we don't belong there, do we? Only sensible thing Aunty May ever said to me. You remember? She said we belong out here in the wilds together. Well, we do, don't we?' The fox sat trim beside him, attentive, alert to every sound of the encroaching night. 'Mind you,' said Billy, 'I could do with some of her baked beans, couldn't you? Wouldn't even say no to a corned beef sandwich, and I know you wouldn't, would you? Yes, you're right. Best not to talk about it, only makes it worse.' But he was too tired even to talk now. He beat the bracken around him into a soft bed, and lay back in it, turned on his side, his knees drawn up to his chin and was asleep almost at once.

But the fox did not sleep, not yet anyway. For him food came before sleep. He went out hunting in the woods just above where Billy lay. He had been hunting before, but it was never as urgent then as it was now. He was slow and inexperienced, but hunger had sharpened his reactions, and after being given the run-around by an irritating fieldmouse that had mastered the art of vanishing, he cornered and at last exhausted a field vole and killed it. But this first kill seemed only to stimulate his appetite. He spent most of the night high up in the woods above where Billy slept, stalking and pouncing ineffectually, trying to repeat his early success; but with the dew coming down in the early morning the worms came wriggling to the surface in the soft earth of the forest tracks and the fox treated himself to a feast of them before he returned to snuggle up tight against Billy's chest. He curled his tail over his nose and slept.

Morning came too soon for both of them. Billy had slept fitfully.

Whichever side he chose to sleep on soon lost all feeling, and the pins and needles that followed were excruciating. When he woke his neck was stiff and he was wet through and shivering with the cold. There were church bells ringing somewhere in the misty valley below him, and a cow lowing mournfully. A persistent invisible pigeon called gently from above him in the trees and a pair of circling buzzards mewed plaintively overhead. Billy watched as a gang of raucous rooks moved in to worry them.

The fox stiffened suddenly beside him at the bark of a dog. Billy was not alarmed for it seemed to him to be harmless enough and still far away. But then there was the murmur of voices, a hooting laugh, and Billy was on his feet and running. He followed the fox up the hillside and into the shelter of the trees. As they ran in under the trees a gunshot blasted behind them and the wood emptied itself noisily of every bird. The fox ran on ahead the way he had gone the night before, and Billy ran after him, stumbling over the dead branches that the fox leapt so easily. Another gunshot echoed along the valley behind them. Billy did not know whether the shots were aimed at them. The fox seemed to know and that was enough for him. Suddenly there were no more trees and Billy was out in the bright sunlight and tearing downhill towards a stream. Beyond the stream was a forest of conifer trees that climbed the hillside in serried lines. There was cover in there. If they could reach the trees Billy felt they had some chance. The fox loped across the open field, hesitated at the stream but then bounded across and up into the trees beyond. Billy splashed through the water after him and plunged into the forest before turning to see if they were being followed. He crouched in the shadows and watched.

Not fifty paces from them two men came out into the field, each of them carrying a gun, a little Jack Russell terrier sniffing the ground around them. 'I saw it,' said one of them. 'Big it was and brown, I saw it, honest. Could've been a deer, even. Gone to cover in the Brigadier's wood. He's got dozens of them in there. He won't notice if there's one missing, will he? Come on, let's go in after him. It's worth a bit, is a deer. Look, the dog's after him, he's got his scent, I told you, I told you.' And sure enough the little Jack Russell was bustling down through the grass towards them, yapping as he came.

Upward was the only way to go. Billy dug his toes into the soft earth and forced his legs to run. The fox needed no whistling on now. He trotted on easily in front, tongue hanging out. They could hear behind them that the hunters were in the woods too, and that the yapping terrier was coming even closer. Billy ran now because the fox ran. He drove himself on, pounding the air with his arms, whispering through gritted teeth, 'Faster, faster, faster. Don't stop. Don't stop.'

With the forest behind them filling with excited voices they reached the forest path at the top of the hill. The fox immediately turned right as if he knew the way, so Billy followed him.

Billy sensed that the fox was leading him somewhere, and he was far too tired to argue. When the fox left the track and bounded up the bank into more trees, Billy clambered after him.

It was a different forest now, with great tall oaks clinging dangerously to the hillside. Many had fallen, their roots ripped out, leaving vast craters where young saplings were sprouting again. As they ran on and up, Billy saw the fox slowing. He was looking around him as he went, no longer intent it seemed on escape. The measured rhythm was gone from his stride and Billy found himself running alongside him, even ahead of him sometimes. Fatigue overcame Billy now as he laboured on, fatigue brought on by the knowledge that he had not thrown off their pursuers. Below in the woods they could hear them crashing through the undergrowth and always that shrill incessant yapping that was leading the hunters inexorably towards them.

The fox had paused by one of the craters, and quite suddenly vanished among the roots. Billy whistled for him

but the fox did not reappear, so Billy
went down into the crater after him.
The earth still clung to the roots that
towered now over Billy, an earth wall
of twisted roots, and at the base of it a
hole that must have been torn out of
the hillside when the tree fell. It
seemed to lead in behind the wall of
roots, and at the mouth of the hole he
saw the white muzzle of the fox. Billy

had no idea how big the hole might be inside, but the hunters were so close now that there was no time for debate. He thrust himself into the hole, arms and head first, but his shoulders stuck fast. He kicked out furiously with his legs and groped in the dark for something on which he could haul himself in, and he found it, a gnarled root that was strong enough to take all his weight. Once inside he looked for the fox and found two eyes staring back at him out of the dark. He gathered the fox to him and crawled to the back of the earth cave and waited. Whatever happened he would never allow the fox to be taken from him.

CHAPTER NINE

The terrier came straight to the hole and would have come in after them had not Billy hurled a clod of earth and stones at his snarling snout. It took a broadside to drive him away and he backed off, yelping in surprise. Billy crouched in the dark with the fox breathing heavily against him, and they heard the hunters' voices as they toiled up the hillside towards the dog that stood quivering and barking at the bottom of the crater.

'Ain't no deer down there. You and your deer, Jack. Run me ruddy legs off I did, and for what?' said one of them. 'Rabbits, that's all there is in there. Came all this way for a ruddy rabbit we did. Lost the scent, didn't he, the useless mutt.'

'He's after something though, isn't he?' said another voice. 'There's a hole down there, see? Big enough for a fox, that is. P'raps it was a fox after all, p'raps he's after a fox. Let's put him in

there and see, eh? We came all this
way, didn't we? Worth a try.' And Billy
heard them slithering down into the
crater. He grabbed the biggest stone he
could find from the floor of the cave
and watched for the terrier's nose to
appear again. But instead of the dog it
was a face they saw, a woolly head of
ginger hair and a red face. 'Pitch black
in there, can't see a thing. Give me the
dog. If anything's in there he'll soon

bring it out. You'll see.'

But nothing would persuade the terrier to put its nose to the hole again. More than once they dragged the wretched animal choking to the mouth of the hole and held it there, pushing it from behind, but the dog dug its front feet into the ground obstinately and backed out yelping just as soon as they let go of his collar. Billy held his fire and hoped.

'There's something in there, got to be. Got to be something in there to make the dog turn tail.'

'He's a useless mutt, Jack, like I said. You should get yourself a proper dog. Yellow as a buttercup he is.'

'Look, if he's frightened, then he's frightened of something, right? So there's got to be something down there, hasn't there? Now if he won't go in after it and drag it out, then we've got to persuade whatever's in there to come out, haven't we?'

'Yeah, but how're we gonna do that, Jack?'

'I'm coming to that. First we got to make sure there isn't another way out of there. We got to block off any other way out. So you get round the other side of that old root and if you find another hole, kick it in so's he can't get out. Then we got him trapped, see?'

Billy listened to the scrambling feet clambering about outside. 'Nothing here,' came a voice from behind the earth wall at the back of the cave. Under Billy's arm the fox licked his lips, gathered his tongue in and listened for a moment, then began to pant in short sharp bursts, every so often pausing to listen again. 'Hey, I think I can hear something. I can, I can. There's breathing inside there.' Billy clasped his hand over the fox's snout to close it and stroked his ears gently to calm him down. 'There's something in there, Jack, I heard it, clear as day. I heard it.'

'If there's something inside there, then it won't want to be there for long. Got a little surprise for it, a nice little surprise. Come back here, and give me a hand. A few twigs and dry leaves—'s all we need.' And Billy heard them climbing up out of the crater sending little avalanches of earth and stones tumbling down behind them, a few of them finding their way into the mouth of the cave.

When the voices were far enough away Billy crawled forward to take a look. There was just a chance, he thought, they might be able to escape before the hunters came back. He could not think why they had gone off to gather twigs and leaves, but whatever it was he did not want to be trapped in that cave when the hunters came back again. When he was sure it was all clear he pushed the fox out in front of him and prepared to follow him out. But the fox seemed reluctant to go and struggled to turn round. As Billy pushed him again, there was a hideous growl and suddenly the terrier was there in front of them, stocky on its four little legs, its lips curled back over its teeth that snapped out its machine-gun rattle of a bark. The fox did not hesitate, he was back through the hole and at the back of the cave before Billy could hurl the stone he still held in his hand. He missed, but it was enough to persuade the terrier to retreat again while he gathered some more ammunition. And then the hunters were coming back, slithering down the slope and laughing as they came.

'All talk, that dog of yours, Jack—all mouth, he is.'

'This'll do the trick, you'll see. Just put it down by the hole there. That's it, a nice pile—only the dry stuff mind you. Don't want anything wet. Now give us that bit of cord you got holding your trousers up.'

'But they'll fall down.'

'Don't matter about that. Who's to see? Come on, give it here. Plenty more of it back at the farm. Can't get a fire lit without it, can we? And it's got to be a good fire. Then we put the leaves on it and push it down that hole and whatever's in there will either be smoked like a kipper or come running out. And when it comes out, which it will, we'll be waiting for it, won't we, to blast it to kingdom come.'

Billy heard a match strike and then the twigs begin to crackle. Then he could smell the smoke. The fox wanted to run and began to struggle. But Billy held on tight. He thought of kicking out the back of the cave but knew it was pointless even to begin. There was no time. The game was up and Billy knew it. He was about to call out and surrender when he heard a different voice outside, the quiet voice of an older man that demanded and was used to instant obedience.

'Put that fire out 'fore you set the whole wood alight, you idiots. Stamp it out I tell you, or I'll get ugly. And you wouldn't like me ugly. I don't even like myself when I'm ugly, so just do as you're told and put out that fire!' The voice rose to a sharp command. There was much scuffling outside in the crater. Billy lowered his head to the floor of the cave and could just see their boots stamping out the last of the fire. 'Very well. That will do. Over here the two of you so you can hear me. I'm not going to say this twice. First, you are trespassing on my land. You know who I am and you know you are trespassing. Second, you are poaching. Why else would you have your guns and that little rat of a dog?'

'Only came after a rabbit, didn't we, Jack?'

'That's all, Brigadier, honest.'

'You even lie badly. Is it likely you would go to all that trouble, come all the way up here, to smoke out a rabbit when there's thousands of them hopping about down in the fields? There's more rabbits this year than there's been for years. It's lucky for you I came when I did, 'cos if you'd have caught what you were after then you'd have been up before the Magistrates Monday morning for poaching. Now this time, and only this time, I'll overlook the trespassing; but if I find you in my woods again I'll get ugly, ugly as sin. Now take that horrible little dog and get yourselves out of here before I change my mind. And one more thing before you go; there's been a swan flying around here the last day or so—seen it myself. Easy things to shoot, swans. If you take a potshot at her, I'll know who it is, remember? If you see it you leave it alone, understand? They're protected, a

protected species swans are; but you're not, so get going before my trigger finger gets twitchy.'

Billy's hunched shoulders relaxed as he heard the hunters running off down the hill, the terrier yapping as they went. But he could see one pair of boots were still in the crater and a stick walking with them, and they were coming towards the hole. There was a sound of sniffing and the light was blocked out by a face peering in at them. 'Can't see you,' said the face, that sported a neat white moustache, 'but I know you're in there. Smell a fox a mile away, I can. 'Spect you're out of that earth over in Innocents Copse— saw you when you were little, six of you there were, weren't there? Dashed lucky for you I came by. Only came this way to find that swan. Saw it come down in the woods this morning— funny place for a swan to come down, I thought. Then I spotted the smoke. Came just in time, didn't I? Come September you'll make fine sport for the hounds. So I'll be seeing you again, my fine foxy friend. I'll be the one on the chestnut mare leading the hunt. First over every fence I am: the Master they call me. Be all in pink so you can't miss me. We'll meet again, you can be sure of that. And don't go getting yourself shot in the meantime will you? Always a pity to waste a good fox.'

The boy and the fox waited all day in their earth cave until the daylight at the entrance began to fail. Billy had made up his mind now that it was dangerous to move by day. In future he would travel only under cover of darkness and find somewhere to lie up during the day. He waited until dark had fallen outside before clambering out of the hole. They climbed up through the woods and out once again into open countryside beyond. He could see the city glittering far away below him and knew that if he turned his back on the lights and kept walking he would be going in the direction he wanted. That night they put many miles between themselves and the city for they were able to walk safely enough along the lanes. On the rare occasions a car did disturb them they could see its headlights coming and had plenty of time to climb a gate or jump into a ditch.

Billy kept the fox on a lead again now, a piece of orange twine he had found by the side of the road—he wanted no repeat of their encounter with the little girl the day before. The fox baulked at it more and more as the night went on, and from time to time would sit down obstinately in the middle of the road and refuse to move. It was no use jerking on the string, and Billy knew that. So Billy would sit down beside him on the road and put an arm around him and talk softly in his ear of the place they were going to, how it would be a wild country where there were no people, where they could be together always and where no one would hunt them because no one would even know they were there. 'And when we get there,' Billy said, 'you'll never have to have a lead on you again—won't be any need for it, will there? And there'll be food enough for us both, I promise you. I'll see to it. Come on now, it's not far. I know you're tired, but after all you got four legs and I got two, so you can only be half as tired as I am. On your feet now.'

CHAPTER TEN

By dawn they were over the hills and dropping down into a broad valley of grey shadows. The river that wound its way along it could be seen only fleetingly, glimpsed through wandering mists. For some time now Billy had been on the lookout for a place they could hide up that day. Lights were coming on in the farmhouses all over the valley and the birds had already finished their dawn chorus when he heard a tractor start up in the farmstead to one side of the road. He spotted its funnel belching black smoke and pulled the fox behind the safety of a hedgerow. The tractor rumbled up the farm track towards them.

Billy watched as the farmer off-loaded the milk churns from the trailer onto the stand by the roadside. As he did so he bumped one of them down too hard and the lid flew off, sloping milk out down the side of the churn. The farmer cursed roundly as he

jumped down off the trailer to recover the lid. Until that moment Billy had not even been thinking about food—he had already accepted that they would be going hungry again that day. But this was an opportunity that was too good to miss. He waited until the tractor had disappeared down the farm track, its trailer rattling behind it. Then he was across the road, hauling the fox

125

along with him. He left the fox sitting by the roadside and jumped up onto the stand. He pulled the lid off one of the churns, dipped his cupped hands into the milk and drank until he could drink no more.

An impatient bark below him reminded him that he was not alone. The churn was heavier than he imagined, but he managed to tip it and fill the lid for the fox who lapped it eagerly, licking it clean before looking up at Billy for more. Billy obliged once again, but in his hurry he tipped the churn just too much this time. Suddenly the churn was leaning too far over and his numb fingers could no longer hold it. The crash and the clatter as it hit the ground echoed down the valley and the churn was thundering down the farm track leaving a great white trail of milk behind it. Billy did not have to tell the fox to run, he was gone already under the gate and it was all Billy could do to catch him and retrieve his lead. The fields round about were too open. They would be spotted, so he pulled

126

the fox down into a field ditch and waited.

Billy peered out through the long grass and could just see the farmer and his wife running up the track. She was stamping her foot with fury. 'I've told you times, Albert, times I've told you. That stand is too small, I said. Only built for ten churns and you've tried to squeeze fourteen on there. Well, what do you expect?'

'I can't understand it,' said the farmer, who had retrieved the rolling churn. 'Can't understand it at all.'

'I've told you, and I've told you,' said the farmer's wife. 'How many times do I have to tell you before you'll listen?'

'I know dear, I know. But . . . no, I won't say it . . . You'll only be cross if I do.'

'No I won't,' she said. 'Look at this milk. It's good money wasted, Albert. Makes me cry to look at it.'

'Well if you're sure you won't be cross, then dear, I was going to say that there's no point in crying over spilt milk.' And she laughed despite herself, chasing the farmer back through the lane, splashing through the elongating puddle of milk as she ran. In his ditch Billy laughed too, laughed till he was weak. The fox looked up at him amazed, but that only made Billy laugh longer and louder.

From the ditch Billy could see a four-bay Dutch barn stacked high with hay, some distance from the farmhouse. The barn, he thought, would be as good a place to sleep that day if they could climb up into it. The barn was only three bays full, and there was a hay elevator standing in the fourth bay. Billy did not like heights but it was getting lighter all the time and there was nowhere else to hide up, so he tucked the fox under his arm and began to climb up. The elevator wobbled dangerously, but he clung on and kept climbing until he reached the top, where he crawled away into the middle of the stack and lay down, exhausted. The corrugated roof was so close above his head he could reach up and touch it. The fox stole about the haystack peering nervously over the edge and then backing away. He seemed interested in exploring, but Billy called him back, and he came willingly enough and lay down beside him and joined him in a deep and untroubled sleep. Neither the prickly hay nor the heavy heat of the haystack disturbed them. Billy was almost roused once by what sounded like a sudden gust of strong wind passing overhead, but it came only as an intermission between dreams and did not wake him.

Voices woke them that evening, voices that Billy recognised at once as the farmer and his wife. 'Got to get it in tonight,' she said. 'They speak of rain before morning.'

'They always speak of rain, dear,' he said. 'It's their job to be gloomy. I'd be happier to leave it till tomorrow and risk it. 'S a bit green that hay, you know. Could do with the sun on it for another day at least I'd say. Don't like to stack hay too green—seen too many of these barn fires in my time. That's what happens if you bring it in too green.' But when she mentioned something about wasted milk and rickety milk stands it was clearly sufficient to change his mind, for the trailer came rocking back and forth all evening, high with its load of hay.

Billy watched anxiously as the hay in the fourth bay began to pile ever higher and higher. It was hot and close under the roof of the barn with little enough air to breathe. He retreated to the darkest corner of the stack and hoped they would not be seen. More help had arrived and there were half a dozen people swarming around the barn as the clouds gathered grey and thick over the trees on the far side of the valley. And all the time the haystack was growing, higher and higher. Any minute now they would reach the top of the stack and Billy and the fox would be spotted. There was nothing for it. He pulled aside a few bales until he had made a trench wide enough and long enough to take the two of them. Then he pulled the bales back over the top leaving only enough of a hole for them to breathe through. Billy peeped out from time to time to keep watch, but once the stack had reached the top in the fourth bay and there were men working on the same level, he dared not even do this, but lay buried in his grave of hay with the fox, sweating till his clothes were wet with it.

Thunder rolled around the skies and ricocheted across the valley and with it came torrential rain drumming with a deafening force on the corrugated roof above them. Within a quarter of an hour all the haymakers had dispersed and Billy thought it safe to push away the covering bales and climb out from his hiding place. He ventured to the edge and found they were alone. Billy sat with his legs dangling out over the edge of the stack and breathed the cooler air outside the barn. As he sat there he saw the first of the lightning crackling in the sky over the darkening valley and he counted the seconds between the thunder and the lightning to see how far away the storm was. One second for one mile, someone had once told him. He counted ten and it was getting closer all the time.

It was the fox who led him to his only food for two days. Absorbed by the storm he had not noticed that the fox had disappeared and when at last he turned round to look for him he saw him stalking low over the hay bales. The hen flew up before the fox sprang and ran away, squawking with terror before taking off into the night. Billy scrambled over the bales on his hands and knees and arrived at the nest of eggs at about the same time as the fox. There were six warm eggs, and Billy shared them out equally, cracking them into his hand so that nothing was wasted. He had never before eaten a raw egg and to begin with he was revolted by the idea, but he watched the fox devour one with relish and followed suit. No egg had ever tasted that good before.

CHAPTER ELEVEN

With a good sleep and a meal inside them at last, they were in high spirits as they climbed down out of the hay barn that night. Billy waited until the worst of the rain had passed and then with a fresh spring in his stride he set off to cross the valley that night. 'Got to cross the river tonight,' he told the fox. 'The further they got to search, the less chance they got of finding us.' But the fox needed no encouragement. He walked on ahead, the lead always at full stretch, pulling Billy along behind him. There was no moon now so Billy could see little except the grey sliver of road in front of him. They left the road when it began to twist uphill and away from the river. Once in the fields again Billy let the fox off the lead.

There were no alarms except for a sheep that coughed from behind a hedge. It was a human cough, a perfect imitation of Aunty May's smoker's cough, and it was enough to send them scurrying into a flooded ditch. And more than once some great white bird wafted by over their heads; a barn owl Billy imagined it to be at first, but then he remembered the barn owl in his Wilderness flew more silently than this one, whose wings whistled gently as they beat the air. Billy thought it must be a bigger barn owl and thought no more about it.

The fox glanced up at it and knew exactly what it was.

They had not gone far that night when the rain began to fall again, a few sparse heavy drops at first, but as the wind got up it lashed down and they were soaked to the skin within minutes. Billy thought of finding somewhere to shelter, but he was determined to cross the river that night, and anyway, he reasoned, he was already as wet as it was possible to be, so what was the point? No, they would battle on through the rain until they reached the river.

And so indeed they did, some hours later. But by this time Billy was shivering with the cold and his legs were numb from the knees down. He was suffering frequent stomach cramps, and knew he could not go on much further. The rain had turned to hail now as Billy skirted the river bank, looking desperately for a bridge across, or for somewhere to hide up. The fox walked alongside him, nose to the ground to avoid the stinging hailstones. He would stop only to shake the wet from his fur, and then he was trotting on again, turning to wait for Billy to catch him up. His companionship that dreadful night kept Billy from giving up. He was always there to talk to, and then whenever they rested for a while under a tree or under the lee of a hedge he would push his head under Billy's arm as if to comfort him.

'Got to be a bridge soon. Got to be,' Billy said, more for himself than for the fox. 'Can't be far now.' It was a hope rather than a promise, but because it was spoken to the only fellow creature he loved in the whole world, it was enough to spur him on, enough to drive him to his feet once more and out into the wild night.

The rain eased at last just before
dawn, the thunder-clouds disappearing
under cover of the night, leaving the
fields sodden and the trees still raining.
Billy and the fox found themselves
starting out across a broad sweep of
flat water-meadows that followed
the winding course of the river
uninterrupted as far as the eye could
see. Still there was no bridge, and
nowhere at all for them to hide out in
the open water-meadows. Even at its

narrowest the river was far too wide for them to swim across, and yet that was just what Billy was contemplating when the fox beside him froze, one paw lifted in the air, his ears pricked. Billy stopped to listen. At first he could hear only the rush of the river and the croaking cry of a rising heron as it lifted out of the reeds nearby. Then through it all, unmistakeable now, though distant, the sound of a strange unearthly music.

Suddenly the fox was no longer by his side. He was running over the field towards the music. Billy called him back, but the fox ignored him. Reluctantly Billy followed, whistling all the while for the fox to stop and come back. Even though he was weak with cold and fatigue Billy had no inclination whatsoever to give himself up, and when he saw the dark silhouette of the barge moored at the bend of the river his instinct was still to hide. The music was warming and welcoming, but it was not that that drew Billy on now towards the barge, it was the sight of his fox sitting down only a few paces from the barge, head on one side, listening to the music. The fox was showing himself quite openly to whoever was on the barge, so Billy thought there was little point in his hiding any more.

As he walked slowly towards the barge Billy noticed that the water around it was alive with birds—moorhens, mallards, herons, a fleet of Canada geese and one large white swan. Every one of them was facing the music, listening intently to it; and in the fields on both sides of the river the cows and the sheep stood quite still, gazing hypnotically at the barge, some of them legless in the low-lying mist.

The dark hulk of the barge took on features as Billy came closer. It was painted from end to end with wreaths of flowers, and perched amongst them, almost hidden, Billy could pick out the shape of swans, dozens of them, wonderfully painted. And sitting in a deckchair by the wheelhouse was a man, dressed, Billy could see, in a collarless shirt, a tatty dark jacket and a wide straw hat with several holes in it. He could not yet see the face for it was bent forward under the shadow of the hat and was covered entirely by two large hands that seemed to massage the music out of the mouth-organ. Only when the tune was finished did the man sit back in his chair and at last look up.

'Christopher! Christopher!' said the man, pushing himself up out of the deckchair and coming towards Billy across the deck of the barge. 'Is it really you?'

'I'm Billy, Billy Bunch,' said Billy, perplexed by the man's question. The man nodded slowly, tried to smile but could not. There was in his eyes the far-away look of a solitary kind of man. Billy decided he was quite old, not yet grandfather old but old none the less. The sad, lined face under the straw hat gave him the appearance of a weary scarecrow that still tried to look the part, but had long ago lost the art of

frightening the birds away. For there was nothing alarming about his dishevelled appearance, nothing wild in his eyes. When he did speak again his voice was firmer and younger, Billy thought, than his looks.

'Caught out in the storm then were you, old son?' the man asked.

'Yes,' said Billy.

'Wet through I shouldn't wonder.'

'Yes.'

'Hungry?'

'Yes.'

'That your fox, is it?'

'Yes.'

'Thought so. Thought so. Better bring him on board then. You've time to dry yourselves off before breakfast. Bacon and eggs it'll be. It's all there is, all I ever have. He'll have eggs and bacon will he?'

'He likes eggs,' said Billy, looking down at the gap of dark water between the barge and the bank. 'How do I get on, anyway?' And as if to show him, the fox leapt nimbly across onto the barge.

'Like that,' said the man and he reached out his hand and Billy took it and jumped on board.

Some way up-river, in sight of the barge, the lone swan sailed in amongst the reeds, waddled awkwardly up onto the bank and began to preen herself, arching her neck and twisting backwards so she could dive her bill amongst the feathers under her folded wings.

CHAPTER TWELVE

That first meal together was eaten almost in silence. Billy was so tired he could not even find the words to thank the man for the food and the dry clothes. Anyway his mind was on other matters—he was desperately trying to dream up a satisfactory story and that was not easy. He was conscious, too, of being watched. Every time he looked up, the man in the battered straw hat seemed to be shaking his head, a rueful smile on his lips as he studied Billy from across the table. It made Billy feel uncomfortable, almost resentful. It was as if the man knew something he didn't know. The smile broke into a laugh for the first time as Billy wiped his lips with the bread, dipped it in his mug of tea and fed the fox that sat patiently beside him. This was the third plate of bacon and eggs the boy and the fox had wolfed down between them, and they had eaten their way through over half a loaf of bread.

In the end it was Billy who spoke first because he wanted to forestall the questions that would inevitably come, and anyway he was ready with his story now. He had thought at one point of telling the man the truth, but he knew that to tell the truth would be the end of everything. He might still be able to bluff it out. 'You live here on this boat, Mister?' he asked.

'Mister?' said the man, laughing. 'Mister? Can't have that. I'm called Joe to my friends. When people are cross with me they call me Joseph. But I'm Joe to you.' He sat back, folded his arms, and considered the boy and his fox in front of him. 'And it's a barge, old son, not a boat. I think it's best not to ask questions, don't you? I mean if I were to ask you now where you've come from and why you're here with that fox, either you wouldn't tell me or you'd make up some story which you'd want me to believe. The trouble with telling someone a story is that it means you don't trust them. So I'm not going to ask you any questions. When you're ready to tell me where you've come from or where you're going to, then I'll listen, I'll be happy to listen. Agreed?' Billy nodded, and set about scraping up the last of the egg yolk on his plate with his last crust.

Billy thought then of using his story, the story about how he was out camping, and this fox had wandered up to his tent one night, and then there was this storm and it blew away the tent and that's how they came to be wandering together down by the river. But as he considered it, he knew it sounded feeble. He was glad not to have to use it.

'Now, old son, clearly you were on the way to somewhere—otherwise you wouldn't have been out in that storm. Question is, am I going your way? Thing is, old son, I've only enough food on this barge for myself, 'cos there's only one of me. Now if you're staying I shall have to go into the village a couple of miles away and get in some food, won't I? Won't take me long— I've got my bike, if you can call it that. Soon as I'm back I'll be moving on down-river.'

145

'Which way's that?' Billy asked. 'Is it away from the city or towards the city?'

'It's that way,' said the man, pointing to the bow of the barge. 'And that's away from the city.'

'Then I'll stay,' said Billy quickly.

'Good,' said the man, standing up, his head almost touching the roof of the galley. 'You've come just at the right time. I was going back down-river anyway today. Got a full house you might say. And old *Noah's Ark* isn't what she was—she takes her time these days. Can't hurry her, you know.'

'Noah's Ark?' said Billy.

'The barge, old son. She's got to have a name, hasn't she?'

'I can only stay if my fox stays with me,' said Billy, putting his arm around the fox. 'We're together, see.'

'I can see that,' said the man, shaking his head again. 'I can see that. Never seen anything like it. Couple of little foxes come in from nowhere. Mind you, I can't have him wandering around below decks, not with the birds. He'll have to stay on deck, just to be safe.'

'Birds?' said Billy. 'What birds?'

'Come on, I'll show you,' said Joe. 'But take that fox back up on deck first of all. You'll see why soon enough.'

The fox seemed content to wander away to the bows of the boat where he sat and surveyed the river around him. Billy went below decks with Joe. The barge was divided in two, with cabin, galley and wheelhouse forward and a long hold aft. They climbed down the stepladder into the hold which was only dimly lit by the light from the portholes. Only when Joe opened the skylight could Billy see that on each side of him were wire cages and that each of them contained a swan, sometimes two.

'Noah's Ark!' said Billy, looking round him. 'That's why you call the ship *Noah's Ark*.'

'Barge,' said Joe, putting an arm round his shoulder.

'What they all in here for?' said Billy. 'Should be outside, on the river. That's where they belong, swans.'

'Most of them will go back there,' Joe said, 'but I'm afraid not all of them.

I s'pose you could call this a hospital barge, Billy,' Joe said, tossing some grain through the bars of a cage. 'See Billy, there's people throw all sorts of rubbish into this river and if it's small enough rubbish it's going to end up down some poor swan's throat. Lead weights—you know, the kind they use for fishing—they've only got to swallow a few of them and they'll die, and die slowly. Often it's too late to do anything for them; but we have to try, don't we Billy? But the worst is people who shoot and miss—most of these in here are recovering from gunshot wounds. There's something about a swan, Billy. I think it's because they're so beautiful, so perfect. People resent that. Perhaps it's a kind of envy. Can't think of any other reason why you'd want to shoot a swan, can you? Then of course there's the young ones that can't look after themselves just yet—maybe the parent birds died or deserted them—so I take them in, feed them up and send them on their way again. Feel I've got to do it for them, Billy. Every year there's fewer of them—I know

148

because I monitor their numbers. Hardly a swan on this river I don't know about. It's my life, Billy. May seem a funny thing to do but the swans on this river mean everything to me.' He spoke with a quiet passion that immediately earned Billy's respect.

By the time they left the hold, Billy knew he had found a friend and rejoiced at it. He climbed up onto the deck of the barge and followed Joe to where the fox lay curled up, half asleep. 'He'll be happy enough up here,' said Billy. 'Only, can I have him sleeping on my bed at night? He won't do any harm, honest.'

' 'Course he can, Billy,' said Joe, lighting his pipe. He looked from the boy to the fox and back again shaking his head in disbelief. 'A couple of little foxes. Never had foxes on *Noah's Ark* before. Took in a half-drowned badger once, and a hedgehog, but never a fox. And now I've got two of them. Two right little foxes.'

Billy and the fox slept all that morning whilst Joe went off on his bone-shaker of a bicycle to buy some food. Joe had lent Billy a pair of huge pyjamas that had to be rolled up at the wrists and ankles to accommodate him. They were heavy and tickly and smelt of pipe tobacco, but that did not trouble Billy—nothing did. Cocooned under a mound of blankets he fell at once into a deep and dreamless sleep.

They were woken some time later by a deep growling vibration that shook the entire barge before the engine coughed, spluttered and at last settled into a rhythmic chug.

It was that slow chug of a heartbeat that propelled the barge down-river at little more than walking pace, a heartbeat that missed a beat every now and again; and whenever it faltered Joe would coax the barge along as if she were a horse. 'Come on. Giddy-up, there's a good girl now. Downhill all the way now girl. Giddy-up now.'

The days on the barge were long and followed a regular routine. Every morning before daybreak Joe would shake him awake and beckon him up on deck, leaving the fox still curled up asleep on his bunk. 'The dawn is the magical time of day,' Joe often told him. 'When you feel you can make things happen just by believing they will. Only your age I was when I learnt to play the mouth-organ and thought that maybe I could sweeten the birds in so that I could see them close to. And it never fails. Sometimes you get a big audience and sometimes just a few. To them it's such a strange sound that they have to come and listen, and to do that they have to come close. And that's my reward, to have them only a few feet away and to watch them watching me.' And as Billy found out each morning it never did fail. The birds were reluctant to begin with. The moorhens would always approach first, but within minutes others would come gliding in from all directions through the still water towards the barge and hover around it like bees around honeysuckle. Either the light of dawn would break the spell or Joe would finally run out of breath and stop playing. Then, the concert over, they would drift away slowly and disperse as if it had never happened. Billy

marvelled at it each time he witnessed it.

Then there were the sick swans to tend to. Every morning before they set off down-river, Joe would take Billy into the hold to feed them. Each cage had to be cleaned out and a bed of fresh straw laid down. As he worked alongside Joe, Billy longed to tell him of the swan he had saved on the canal, but he dared not for he knew if he once began he would have to tell him the whole story and he was not yet ready to risk that.

For most of the day the fox lay curled up in the sunshine in the bows of the barge and Billy would sit beside him, his legs dangling over the side waiting for the next lock to come into view, for it was at the locks that Billy really came into his own. Joe would steer the barge close enough to the bank for him to leap out onto the towpath. Then he would race on ahead and try to swing open the lock gates before *Noah's Ark* arrived so that Joe could glide her into the lock without having to stop. The locks were Billy's responsibility and he warmed to the task with each day that passed.

Each evening at dusk, when the barge was tied up and they had had their supper, Billy would take the fox for a long run out into the countryside. Chasing each other around the thistles in the meadows until Billy flopped to the ground to rest; but the fox would have none of it, tugging at his trousers until Billy had to get to his feet and the game would go on, and on. And finally, when both of them could run no longer, they would wrestle together on the ground, the fox only happy to end the game when he was standing over Billy, his tongue hanging down and panting in his triumph.

Joe sat on the barge smoking his pipe to keep the midges away and wondered at the two of them. The boy had talked of little else but the fox since the first day they had met, and he would talk about him not at all as if he were a pet, but as a friend and a best friend at that. As Joe watched he feared for the future, for he knew a fox would always be a fox.

CHAPTER THIRTEEN

One evening the fox did not come back to the barge after their romp in the grass. Billy searched in the dark for an hour, shining the torch out over the fields, scanning the night for the glinting eyes of a fox. But he found only the yellow eyes of sheep shining back at him, and never the glazed red of the fox. 'Maybe he'll be back by morning, Billy,' said Joe. 'Gone hunting, perhaps.'

'He can't hunt,' said Billy. 'He's too young. He'll starve out there on his own, I know he will.'

'Then perhaps he's out there learning, Billy. He has to learn to hunt if he's ever going to live alone in the wild.'

'But he's not,' Billy cried. 'He's going to stay with me, for always.'

'Billy, old son,' said Joe. 'You know a fox is a wild animal. I don't know how you got hold of him, but I bet you got him from the wild, and a fox will always go back to the wild in the end, Billy. You can't keep a fox tame for ever.'

All that night Billy thought of what Joe had said. Until then it had simply never occurred to him that the fox might ever want to leave him, and when he woke in the early hours of the morning and found the fox asleep on the bunk beside him, he felt like shouting with joy and waking Joe just to tell him that his fox had come back, that he was right after all, that he would never go off and leave him. But he waited until breakfast and said it then. Joe lit his first pipe of the day and sighed. 'Billy, old son, I've been looking after wild things all my life. To start with I wanted to possess every one of them, to collect them, to keep them by me so that I could look at them. You learn, old son, that you can't do it, not if you want to do your best by them. This morning I'm going to release two of our swans—you know, the ones that had their legs tangled up and torn by the fishing line. I don't want to see them go, but I've done all I can for them. Now it's up to them. Maybe

they'll live—I hope so—and maybe they won't; that's not in my hands. Just because I helped them, Billy, they don't belong to me. They're wild, Billy. You told me yourself, remember? It's where they belong, out there on the river. And the longer you cling on to your fox, old son, the harder it will be for him to turn wild again. The younger he goes, the more chance he has of surviving out there.' Billy knew he was right, but could not bring himself to acknowledge it openly.

'He's my fox,' he said, 'and we're together. He don't want to run off, else why's he come back?'

'One day he may not, old son,' said Joe, and left it at that.

Each evening now the fox would disappear earlier and come back later at night, once so late that Billy was out on deck at dawn listening to Joe playing his mouth-organ, when the fox came trotting back across the field and sat down at some distance from the barge to listen. He would rarely come now when he was called, and instead of curling up beside Billy in the bows of the barge he would pace the decks like a caged tiger. When he was with Billy he seemed no less fond of him, no less trusting, but Billy sensed the fox was becoming more and more distant, more and more interested in other things.

On that last evening they were sitting out on deck, and Billy had his arm around the fox. He could feel the fox pulling away from him but held on, reluctant to let him go in case he did not come back. 'Billy, old son,' said Joe. 'That fox sitting beside you is a wild fox. He loves you, Billy, as much as you love him. He loves you like a mother, Billy. But foxes leave their mothers, old son. If he comes to rely on you he won't be a real fox any more, you'll have taken away his wildness, Billy, and that would be a terrible thing, almost like taking his soul away from him. Let him go, Billy. Let him go, old son.'

Billy released his hold on the fox and immediately the fox leapt for the shore and ran off. Joe and Billy waited on the deck until the night settled black about them before going to bed.

Billy did not even call for the fox that night, he knew by now that there was no point. He knew he was losing him. It was a hot night, too hot to sleep, and anyway half of him was always awake waiting for the fox. It was that night that he told Joe all about Aunty May and all the other aunties and uncles he had had. He told him everything there was to tell, for it was easier to talk in the dark. He told him about the swan, about the lucky grey feather he kept under his pillow, about his stutter, about Mr Brownlow and about the Wilderness, and all about the four fox cubs he had tried to keep alive. Joe listened in silence and never said a word when he had finished except: 'Goodnight Billy, old son.'

The fox was not back by first light nor by breakfast time. Billy could eat no breakfast that morning. Much against Joe's advice he went out into the fields calling and whistling for him to come. When he returned to the barge Joe could see the boy had been crying. Nothing would comfort him and Joe knew it, so he did not attempt it. As he watched the boy sitting dejected in the bow of the barge waiting for the fox, Joe made up his mind what he would do.

He was sure that the fox would come back eventually, and so he did, at about midday, padding across the field towards them. Joe saw it first and had his gun ready to hand. He waited until it was close enough before firing both

barrels of his shotgun in the air above the fox. Billy was on his feet and screaming at Joe to stop shooting, but Joe loaded again and fired over the fox's head. The fox turned and ran for about twenty paces and then stopped again. 'It's the only way, Billy,' said Joe, loading the gun once again. 'The fox has only one enemy, Billy; man, you and me. If you want him to survive out there, then it's a lesson you'll have to teach him yourself.' He handed Billy the gun. 'Fire into the sky, Billy. Frighten him so he'll never come back. Do it Billy, do it for him, and do it now.'

Billy pulled the trigger twice and watched the fox bolt across the field and vanish into the trees.

CHAPTER FOURTEEN

For some days after that Billy would neither speak nor eat. He sat in the bows of the barge, his grey feather in his hand, his eyes scouring the countryside round about for the fox. Joe left him alone with himself. He knew there was nothing he could say that would not sound trite, so he preferred to say nothing until the wound had begun to heal, as he knew it would.

Billy was sitting out on deck that last night on the barge, trying to drag his soul out of the darkness. He knew Joe was not to blame, that he ought to speak to him, that the right thing had been done, but he could not bring himself to say anything. When Joe came and sat beside him, puffing on his pipe, Billy looked away. 'Billy, old son,' he said. 'Only last year something happened to me that made me feel just like you feel now. It made me feel that life was unfair and cruel, that the world

163

was a terrible place where I did not belong. They were black days, Billy, but I had a friend, a dear friend, who made me see that it was worth going on, that the swans still needed to be cared for, that life had to be lived. You have to look at it this way, Billy, old son. That fox is out there right now where he should be, and he's there because you kept him alive against all the odds. That's your reward, Billy, old son.' And when Joe put his arm around Billy's shoulder, Billy could cry as he had needed to all that time, all those ten long years.

The next day they were cruising down a broad stretch of river, passing an island that was white with swans. They were travelling faster than usual for some reason, engine at full throttle, when suddenly the engine died, leaving them floating silently towards the bank. As the barge slowed, pushing into the reeds, Joe shouted to Billy to jump off and tie up.

'Sounds bad,' he said. 'Poor old girl—she's just about due for retirement. Built her myself, Billy, my

164

father and I did. Nearly forty years old she is. I'll have a look below—see if I can fix her. Tie her up properly fore and aft, won't you Billy. Wouldn't want to drift on this stretch with no engine.' And he lifted the engine hatch and peered into it, shaking his head. Time after time he tried to start her up but the engine never even gave so much as a hopeful cough. He rubbed his hands with an oily rag. 'It's no good, Billy old son,' he said, 'she's had it. Needs help if we're going to get her started again. Still, if we've got to break down somewhere I suppose this isn't a bad spot to do it. See that house up there across the fields—must be a telephone in a place like that. Come on.'

They walked from the river, along an avenue of lime trees that led to an ancient red-brick house with gabled roofs and stone mullion windows. There was a huge pond with wonderfully coloured ducks swimming around in it, and the hedges on either side were clipped out like great birds, pheasants, cockatoos. And there were roses, roses everywhere. 'Big, isn't it?'

said Billy. 'Like a palace. Wouldn't want to clean the windows in this place.' But Joe said nothing. He seemed suddenly tense, almost excited. They crossed the deep crunchy gravel and walked up the steps to the huge oak front door that was studded with nails. But to Billy's amazement Joe did not knock on the door at all but walked straight in. He threw his straw hat onto a chair and ushering Billy in front of him, marched through the hallway into a huge sitting room where there were paintings as big as the walls in Billy's bedroom back at Aunty May's. There were two people in the room, a smiling policeman with three stripes on his arm, standing with his back to the fireplace, his hands behind his back. And sitting in an armchair beside him was a lady who got up as they came into the room. Billy sensed some kind of trap and backed away. But Joe took his hand gently and led him in.

'Well, here he is, dear,' said Joe, kissing the lady fondly on both cheeks. 'I brought him home, just like you wanted me to. This is Billy Bunch. Billy old son, I want you to meet Molly.'

'You married then?' Billy asked, looking up at Joe, and Joe nodded.

'Hallo Billy,' she said, as she kissed him on both cheeks. The lady did not have to bend down far for she was short. Her hair, which was greying at the temples, was drawn up behind her in a plait and pinned to the top of her head. She smelt of flowers and wore no make-up and Billy liked that. 'Joe's told me so much about you, I feel I know you quite well already.' Billy had a hundred questions, but there was no time to ask even one.

'And Billy,' said Joe, 'this is Police Sergeant William Fazackerly. Now he has his own very special reason for wanting to help you. And he has been a great help, Billy, sorted it all out with the Social Services people. They know you're here, Billy. You see, old son, I knew who you were that first morning when you came to the barge. Not at first, I didn't. At first I thought you were someone else—but I'll tell you about that in a minute, Billy. You were in all the papers, Billy, on the radio.

Everyone was on the lookout for you. Luckily Sergeant Fazackerly here had visited my barge the day before. They knew you were heading in the direction of the river; asked me to keep a lookout for you. So I was half expecting you to turn up, and when you did I rang the Sergeant from the village that same morning, told him I'd found you and that they could call off the search; and I told him I'd look after you till I got home. After that I rang Molly here and I told her all about you and she thought what I thought, that some things are meant to be. She told me to bring you home. So I did and here we are.'

'You live here? In this place? You don't live on the barge?' Billy asked, trying to piece it all together.

Joe shook his head and smiled. 'So you see I knew all about you, old son, even before you told me yourself, but I was glad you did that, old son, very glad. You don't know about us though, do you Billy? Well, maybe it's time I told you. It all happened about a year ago, Billy. It was early springtime, Billy,

and we'd found four little cygnets high
and dry after a flood, no parent bird
around. My son, Christopher—he was
about your age—he fed them and
looked after them for a few weeks, and
then when they were ready to fly we
decided to release them. We ringed
them as we always do the young ones
and took the barge upstream for a few
miles to get them away from the
swannery on the island—didn't want to
risk them being attacked by the adult
birds. We were two days up-river,
weren't we, Molly, and Christopher
was releasing them from the bank. I
was busy tinkering with the engine;
Molly was in the galley. When I went
up on deck later the four cygnets were
swimming away but there was no sign
of Christopher. We don't know how it
happened even now, Billy, but they
found him downstream later that day,
drowned. That was the great sadness I
told you about on the barge, Billy. It
was the same for you when you lost
your fox. Soon as I saw you that
morning, Billy, soon as I knew it wasn't
Christopher walking across the field

towards me, I thought to myself that providence had smiled on us and was giving us back a son. We need you, old son, Molly and me, every bit as much as you need us. We know we get on, don't we; we love the same things. And if you get on with me, you'll get on with Molly. Molly wants to be your mother, Billy, and I want to be your father, if you'll have us.'

Sergeant Fazackerly looked at the boy. 'Well, Billy Bunch,' he said. 'Can I tell the office you'll be staying here with these good people?'

'For good?' Billy asked. 'Do you mean for ever?'

'We mean for ever, Billy,' said Joe, putting his arm around his wife. Molly nodded. 'For ever, Billy,' she said.

'Take it or leave it, son,' said Sergeant Fazackerly. 'I know what I'd do.'

'I'll take it,' said Billy. And he put his hand in his pocket to find his feather, but it was gone. 'Must have dropped my lucky feather,' he said.

'Won't need it any more, will you?' said Joe. 'Not any more.'

171

If any of them had looked out of the window at that moment they would have seen a solitary swan standing by the duck-pond, looking up at the house. Round her left leg she wore a red plastic ring. She waddled towards the pond and settled into the water, frightening the ducks out of the pond. Then she was taking off, her wings beating the water behind her, her legs paddling the water, lifting her high into the air down the lime avenue towards the swannery, all her debts paid, her mission accomplished at last.